MATTHEW MCLACHLAN IS AN award-winning playwright. He was born in Scotland, raised in Florida, and currently survives in New York City.

Another Collection of One Acts

AND MORE THINGS YOU MAY OR MAY NOT ENJOY

• • •

Matthew McLachlan

ISBN: 979-8-3525-6099-0

For Mutt—
The best grandmother in the world who would've kicked my ass
for calling her "grandmother." Miss you every day.

Contents

Preface

● ● ●

IT'S BEEN SIX YEARS SINCE I published the first collection of one acts, and I still suck at writing about myself and my writing. Okay, maybe I'm *better*, but I still don't like it. Give me an hour and I will write you the best, weirdest, funniest damn one act you've ever *seen*! Give me two weeks to write this exact preface and I will have two weeks' worth of plays read, videogames played, and some hilarious and treasured memories made with friends…but no preface. Luckily, I've picked up some helpful phrases I've heard people say about my work over the years, so I just recycle those whenever I need to talk about it. There's one word that I've heard most often when people describe the stories I tell that's stuck out: *universal.*

When I first heard that, I thought, "*Universal*? What does that mean? Is my writing vague? Do I need to be more specific?" It wasn't until a friend said, "No, dummy, it means you're writing about stuff that *everyone* relates to. The human aspect in everyone." Oh. Okay. Well, that sounds good. But it wasn't until I was adding in the character descriptions in this book and found that almost all of the monologue descriptions say, "Any age. Any gender," that I might have actually considered what my friend said to be true. And this isn't me tooting my own horn here.

I'm just happy I have a way to describe my work that I'm proud of. That I can truthfully say that what I need to write and want to live through is seen, felt, and understood by most everyone who reads it (which feels good because it took me a long time to write what I *needed* to write).

Story time: A few years ago, I was lucky enough to have lunch with and pick the brain of one of the biggest playwrights in the biz. We were in a one act festival together, struck up a conversation afterward, and agreed to grab lunch. I must've felt extra bold that day because before I left, I gave him a copy of my first collection of one acts. A week later and halfway through the lunch, he said, "I read some of your work." *Wait. Really?* "You like a good *premise*, don't you?" Now, *normally*, I probably would've choked on my razor-sharp turkey melt panini right there in the middle of fancy-pants Brooklyn. Luckily for me, I had this exact realization about my work a few weeks prior. What he meant was, I wrote a lot of stuff that had a great outer shell—a sleek-looking vehicle but no real engine. Nothing driving it forward. No "why."

Maybe that was a harsh thing to say outright, but hey, he wasn't wrong. My work *didn't* have any personal reason why. It was all for a laugh or just a good or interesting idea. Now that's not true about *everything* I wrote up until that point, but it was true for most of it. So I swore from that moment on to never write anything that didn't have a solid reason why or didn't feel deeply personal to me. Sure, I can come up with an amusing or interesting premise all the livelong day, but if it doesn't have a reason why, I don't bother. Here's an example: in here, you'll read the incredibly silly one act called *Toxic Norse-culinity* about Vikings learning to shed their toxic masculinity. At first I just liked the idea of two Vikings talking in Viking-speak with a regular guy named Kevin. Funny idea, but nothing moving it forward. But then I watched the show *Vikings* and saw how toxic the men were in this time and how, even though outlandish, it wasn't too far off from the world we live in today. Oooh, okay, so I can use my silly idea to make a statement about modern-day masculinity and how to live your truth, no matter how "unmasculine" it may be. Boom. Reason why. And that's how I've written my work ever since. You'll even find a one act in here about characters trying to figure out the play they're in, all to discover you need a solid reason *why* something is written and not just have silly and wacky stuff happen on stage. I'm so clever.

In the last six years, I have been in and out of theatre companies, relationships, and probably my mind, but I've always had my writing. Through it, I've made some incredible new lifelong friends and colleagues, shared my work, had experiences with artists I've only ever dreamt of meeting, and had a deep sense of purpose and happiness because I do what I love every day. What you have in your hand is a chunk of a very new me as a person and writer. Yes, there's still some deep silliness throughout, but there's a lot more heart and vulnerability here as well. I am excited to share it all with you. Whether you read the first collection or not, I am forever grateful that you decided to pick up this book and give it a chance—another little collection that you may or may not enjoy.

One Acts

• • •

Guardian

• • •

Production History

Guardian was first performed at Tada! Youth Theatre in March 2018. It was directed by Joshua Warr.

DERRIK: Kirk Koczanowski
GABE: Maki Borden

Guardian was later performed at the Tada! Youth Theatre in June 2019. It was directed by Ann Cooley and produced by Nylon Fusion Theatre Company.

DERRIK: Andrew Maclarty
GABE: Eric Svendsen

CHARACTERS

DERRIK: Late 20s/early 30s. Male.
GABE: Any age. Male.

SETTING
Outside a café.

NOTES
A "/" indicates when the next character begins their line.

DERRIK sits at a table for two. He wears a padded neck brace, a cast on his right arm, and a leg brace on his left leg. A crutch lies next to his chair on the ground. He anxiously fidgets in his seat, blowing on his Starbucks coffee cup, checking his watch. After a while, something in the distance catches his eye.

DERRIK: What the... (*Eyes wide*) Oh, shi—

DERRIK scoots his chair back as GABE, who has large, feathered wings, LITERALLY flies in from offstage, slowly spinning as he does so. His back slams into the table and chair with a loud WHAM! He lands flat on his stomach.

GABE: (*Groaning*) Oooh, my *spiiine*.
DERRIK: Jesus *Christ*, Gabe!
GABE: (*Strained*) "He who is risen."
DERRIK: You almost plowed right into me!

GABE slowly gets to his hands and knees, pulls the chair out, and sits in it, groaning as he does. He wears big, dark sunglasses.

DERRIK: What'd we say about you coming in hot like that?
GABE: It wasn't my fault, okay?! It was the frickin'... (*Points up, angrily*) Wind! Ya know?! Shot me straight down!
DERRIK: I don't feel any wind, Gabe.
GABE: Well, *Derrik*, that's because you're on the ground! In the sky it feels like a fuckin' typhoon, okay?
DERRIK: (*Sighs*) Okay.

GABE: Ev'rybody talks about lightning and snow and shit, but no one ever talks about how bad wind can fuck you up! Even for us angels it can be a bitch!

DERRIK: (*Unconvinced*) Sure.

GABE: *Wind*! I'm tellin' ya!

DERRIK: So, there's absolutely nothing else inhibiting your flight today.

GABE: …Nope.

DERRIK: Nothing at all?

GABE: I mean…there were some geese and shit up there in their little V-shape thing. But I just went right through those fuckers, so…didn't hinder me any.

DERRIK: I can *smell* the booze on you from here, Gabe.

GABE: I may still be a little drunk from last night, there is that.

DERRIK: Jesus Christ.

GABE: (*Flatly*) "He who is risen." Okay, look, I admit…I am not exactly running on one hundred percent today, alright?

DERRIK: Yeah, well…that makes two of us.

GABE sees DERRIK in all of his braces for the first time.

GABE: Good Creator above, what happened to *you*?!

DERRIK: That…is a great question, Gabe.

GABE: *Yes*, yes, it is! 'Cause you look like shit. *Mangled* shit!

DERRIK: Thanks.

GABE: (*Chuckling*) Whatjya…whatjya do? Get trampled by an elephant or something?

DERRIK: *Horse*, actually.

GABE: …What?

DERRIK: I was trampled by a horse.

GABE stares at DERRIK. He slowly lifts his hand to his mouth.

DERRIK: Yeah, sure. Hilarious.

GABE: No, it's just…how is that even possible?! You live in the city!

DERRIK: (*He's told this story a million times*) A horse broke free from one of those horse buggy things and ran into the park. Where I was napping.

GABE: And it just—

DERRIK: Trampled me, yes.

GABE: (*Laughs*) Divine Creator! That's insane! Was anyone else hurt?

DERRIK: (*Annoyed*) Nope.

GABE: You were the only one.

DERRIK: *Yes.*

GABE: Wow. Bad luck, huh?

GABE pulls a flask from out of his feathers and unscrews the top.

DERRIK: *No*, it's — (*Takes breath*) That's actually why I wanted to talk to you.

GABE: Why? You need money?

DERRIK: What?

GABE: For your hospital bills or somethin'?

DERRIK: No, I don't need/*money.*

GABE: 'Cause us angels don't have a need for worldly things like that.

GABE takes a sip from the flask.

DERRIK: (*Ignoring this*) I wanted to talk to you because I was severely *injured*, Gabe.

GABE: ...Okay?

DERRIK stares at GABE, waiting for him to get it.

GABE: And?

DERRIK: *And*! You're my *guardian angel*!

GABE: Ooh, okay, *I* see what you're getting at here. This is somehow *my* fault.

DERRIK: How is this *not* your fault?!

GABE: I'm not the one who was napping in a park like a homeless person!

DERRIK: Other people were napping in the park and they got away just fine! Obviously *their* guardian angels did their job! You did not!

GABE: (*Eye-roll*) My "job."

DERRIK: Yes! Your job! Your entire existence is to prevent my injury! That is your *only* job! Or at least it was.

GABE: Okay, let me tell you some—wait...what?

DERRIK: That's...why I asked you here.

GABE: Wait a second, wait...(*Beat*) Are you...are you *breaking up* with me?

DERRIK: (*Confused*) Is that...what it's called?

GABE: Of course!

DERRIK: Okay, it just...seems a little...*personal*.

GABE: We've been bonded since your life *began*, Derrik! Of course it's/personal!

DERRIK: Okay! I just thought you'd say "fired" or something.

GABE: This is just...(*As if a curse word*) Holy *Father*!

DERRIK: (*Diplomatic*) Now, I'm not really sure of the policies here or…how this works. If you have to find your own replacement or what but—

GABE: Oh! Oh, yes! I'll just send out an *email-blast* across the heavens! See who can cover my shift for the rest of your life! (*Throws up hands*) I just…I can't believe this!

DERRIK: Really, Gabe? Is this really that hard to believe?

GABE: What's that supposed to mean?

DERRIK: Oh, come on! You have been a *terrible* guardian angel!

GABE: That's…*no*, I…I've…done pretty good!

DERRIK: Oh, yeah? I have broken over *twenty-seven* bones in my life. Some more than once! I have to take public transportation everywhere I go because I have been in more car accidents than a *crash-test dummy*! And for as long as I can remember, every flying object ever seems to be a magnet for my *face*!

GABE: Okay. I admit…I have not been the most proactive in my position as guardian.

DERRIK: You never show up! And when you do, you're always wasted!

GABE: There have been a few times that I wasn't!

DERRIK: (*Palm to face*) Jesus Christ.

GABE: "He who is risen." Come on, Derrik! You can't just replace me like this! I mean…it's *me* we're talking about here! We've been together since you were born!

DERRIK: Yes, and my entire life has been one big accident and injury, one after another. It's always been "Derrik's a klutz" or "Derrik's accident-prone," when in reality, it's just been *your* carelessness! So, if I can get someone else who will actually take this job seriously, who will take my *life* seriously, then…I'm going to. I'm sorry, Gabe, but I've gotta be realistic here.

GABE leans back in the chair. He nods, slowly.

GABE: …Realistic.

Silence. DERRIK shifts in his seat, feeling guilty.

GABE: (*Calmly*) Do you know what I did before I was a guardian angel, Derrik?

DERRIK: (*Confused*) I…didn't know guardian angels *could* do something else.

GABE: Oh, yeah. *I*…was a motherfuckin' *archangel*.

DERRIK: (*Unsure*) …No way.

GABE: Yup. Top tier badass with armor, sword, and everything.

DERRIK: …Whoa.

GABE: And ya know what? I was a damn good one too.

DERRIK: Really?

GABE: *Heaven*-yeah! You shoulda seen me during Lucifer's rebellion, man! I was casting out bitches left, right, and center! Ain't nobody cast out as many betrayers as I did! *Nobody*. (*Smiling*) *I*…was the *shit*. Even the motherfuckin' *Seraphim* wanted to hang out with me!

DERRIK: (*Gently*) …What happened?

GABE: After the war was over…I just…wasn't the same. It really messed me up. (*Sad laugh*) I bet you never thought angels could get PTSD, huh? I was temporarily demoted to "regular" angel, which meant delivering boring-ass messages to mortals on the divine Creator's behalf. But I fucked *that* up when I drunkenly told Abraham, as a *joke*, to...ya know...

DERRIK: *You* told him to sacrifice his only son?

GABE: As a *joke*! I didn't think he'd actually *try*! From there I was demoted even further to "guardian." And for almost two millennia, I have spent my days drowning my misery and reminiscing on the good old days...

DERRIK: ...Damn.

GABE: Yeah.

Silence. DERRIK doesn't know what to say.

GABE: Listen, Derrik...I know I've been a shit guardian. And if I'm gonna be honest here, before I was assigned to you, I told myself that the next mortal I got, I was just gonna kick it. Sit back, take it easy, and wallow in my sorrows. *But...* (*Desperate*) If you request a new guardian...I'd be *fucked*, man! I don't even know *what* they'd do. There's never been an angel that's fucked up as badly as I have! I could be the first angel in existence that gets *uncreated*! Not even Lucifer got that! He just got thrown into a dimension with shitty AC!

DERRIK: I get that, Gabe...but what am I supposed to do?

GABE: Just...gimme one more shot!

DERRIK: (*Unsure*) I don't know, Gabe.

GABE: Just one! And if I am not the best guardian angel you've ever seen, you can request a replacement! No argument from me! I promise! Just...gimme another chance. *Please*?

DERRIK studies GABE, who stares at him desperately, genuinely.

DERRIK: (*Sighs*) ...Okay.

GABE: *Yes*! Thank the Creator! That's...that is *great* news, Derrik!

DERRIK: But just one shot!

GABE: Of *course*! That's all I ask! I—oh, man—I won't let you down!

DERRIK: *Okay.* I hope not.

GABE: Oh, you don't need to hope, buddy. I have *got* you! C'mon, I'll take you home.

DERRIK: Yeah, okay.

GABE: Great! We'll even get ice cream on the way! You want some ice cream?

DERRIK: (*Pleasantly surprised*) Um...sure.

GABE: Perfect!

GABE stands up and goes to DERRIK. GABE picks up DERRIK'S crutch and hands it to him.

GABE: I'm not gonna let you get even so much as a brain-freeze, mah man!

DERRIK: (*Impressed*) Okay.

GABE helps DERRIK up.

GABE: There ya go. Nice and easy.

DERRIK stands up, crutch under his arm.

GABE: *There.* (*Beat*) Hey, uh...Derrik?

DERRIK: Yeah?

GABE: …Thanks.
DERRIK: (*Smiling*) …You're welcome.

A moment.

GABE: Alright. 'Nuff fartin' around. Let's get that ice cream!

They turn to leave. GABE sees DERRIK'S coffee.

GABE: Oh! Don't forget this guy!

GABE grabs the coffee as DERRIK takes a hobbled step toward GABE.

GABE: Here ya go!

GABE spins around to hand the coffee to DERRIK but smashes it into DERRIK'S chest, the burning liquid exploding all over DERRIK'S body and face.

DERRIK: YAAAHHH!!!

BLACKOUT.

END OF PLAY.

What the Psychic Said

• • •

PRODUCTION HISTORY

What the Psychic Said was first performed at the Chain Theater in July 2022 for The Chain Theater's Summer One Act Festival. It was directed by David Zayas, Jr.

YOUNG MAN: Marc Reign
YOUNG WOMAN: Kaylee Costello

CHARACTERS

YOUNG MAN: Bright, optimistic, and a hopeless romantic.
YOUNG WOMAN: Confident, to the point, and has nothing
 better to do.

SETTING
A place you can eat your lunch and not be bothered…usually.

NOTES
A "/" indicates when the next character begins their line.

YOUNG MAN stands, out of breath, an opened green juice in his hand, in front of YOUNG WOMAN who sits at a table in the middle of eating a healthy lunch bowl or salad. She stares up at YOUNG MAN, a fork with food on it in hand. They stare at each other, YOUNG MAN with a starry-eyed grin, YOUNG WOMAN extremely confused.

YOUNG WOMAN: …Are you *high*?

YOUNG MAN: No, I'm not high.

YOUNG WOMAN: This sounds like something people say when they're high.

YOUNG MAN: I know it does, but I promise you I'm not.

YOUNG WOMAN: Okay, well, then if this is some kind of joke, I guess I don't really like…*get it.*

YOUNG MAN: It's not a joke, I swear.

YOUNG WOMAN: (*Realizing*) Oh, God.

YOUNG MAN: What?

YOUNG WOMAN: This is just…

YOUNG MAN: What?

YOUNG WOMAN: (*Annoyed*) Are you hitting on me right now?

YOUNG MAN: *What?*

YOUNG WOMAN: Like, is this some new *avant-garde* way guys try to pick up women these days?

YOUNG MAN: I'm not hitting on/you!

YOUNG WOMAN: 'Cause I'll tell you right now, it isn't working, dude.

YOUNG MAN: I'm *not* hitting on you, I swear!

YOUNG WOMAN: …You're serious.

YOUNG MAN: *Yes.*

YOUNG WOMAN: …Okay…so…just so we're… (*Beat*) You're saying that…you saw me sitting here…and are convinced that we're going to spend the rest of our lives together because—and this I really wanna get right—a *psychic* told you this would happen?

YOUNG MAN: Pretty much, yeah.

YOUNG WOMAN: …And you're *sure* you're not high?

YOUNG MAN: Look, I know this sounds kinda crazy—

YOUNG WOMAN: It sounds batshit *bonkers* is what is sounds like.

YOUNG MAN: Right. Yes. But, if you just let me explain, I promise it won't sound so crazy.

YOUNG WOMAN: I doubt that.

YOUNG MAN: Hey, *I* never believed in this stuff either, okay? But things she predicted have *happened*! I mean, very *specific* things! And I know some random guy coming up to you and saying all this is super weird and kinda creepy, but I just…I *saw* you here and I…I needed to… (*Sighs*) Will you just let me explain? Please? Let me explain, and if by the end you still think this is…what did you say? Batshit bonkers? Then, I'll leave you alone and…you'll never see me again. Okay?

YOUNG WOMAN studies him.

YOUNG WOMAN: …*Fine*. But if this turns into you just hitting on me, I'm stabbing you with my fork.

YOUNG MAN: Yeah! Sure! Totally!

YOUNG WOMAN: …Okay.

YOUNG MAN: (*Nodding*) *Okay. Yeah.* So, um…like I said, I never really believed in this stuff, right? But all my friends and family started seeing psychics for some reason, like, that's the new *thing*, I guess. It's all they ever talk about. So, I figured, why the hell not, ya know? Let me just do it so I can say I did it. So, I go, and I'm waiting for this person to be all kooky with sage and crystals and stuff, but she was really kinda...*normal*. For the first fifteen minutes, we just talked about life and stuff, and before I knew it, she's saying things about me that I haven't even *mentioned* yet. Like, about my *job* and where I *live* and stuff!

YOUNG WOMAN: How do you know she didn't just look you up on Facebook or LinkedIn or something?

YOUNG MAN: I thought about that. But I was a walk-in! She couldn't have done all that while we were talking the whole time!

YOUNG WOMAN: (*Skeptical*) Hmm.

YOUNG MAN: So, we're talking for a bit and then she gets very serious and says, "Now, there are a few big things that are going to happen to you this year that are really going to bring you down. Something in *March* and something in *June*." And I'm thinking, "Okay, *that's* pretty specific, right?" Like, if these things *don't* happen, then I *know* she's full of it. But then—

YOUNG WOMAN: Let me guess, something happened in March.

YOUNG MAN: (*Wide eyed*) *Yes*!

YOUNG WOMAN: Okay, see, I have a problem with this already.

YOUNG MAN: What? Why?

YOUNG WOMAN: 'Cause what you're doing is creating a self-fulling prophecy.

YOUNG MAN: Whaddya mean?

YOUNG WOMAN: If she *told* you something was gonna happen, you're either gonna make it happen by obsessing too much or blow some little thing out of proportion that you wouldn't have otherwise and say it was a big thing.

YOUNG MAN: My appendix burst.

YOUNG WOMAN: …*Oh.*

YOUNG MAN: Yeah.

YOUNG WOMAN: Okay, well…that's—

YOUNG MAN: Kind of a big thing?

YOUNG WOMAN: Yes, that…yeah.

YOUNG MAN: Exactly. So, once *that* happened, I was like, "Well, what the hell is gonna happen in *June*?" I'm telling you, I made more doctor's appointments in those next few months than I ever had in my entire life. That way, when June rolled around, I was, like, *ready*, ya know? If something big was gonna happen, I was *ready*! And then on the *very* last day in June…I lost my job! I mean, how do you explain that?

YOUNG WOMAN: Maybe you went to too many doctor's appointments.

YOUNG MAN: Our company was acquired and they laid off half the staff.

YOUNG WOMAN: Whoa.

YOUNG MAN: *See*? These are things I couldn't *make* happen!

YOUNG WOMAN: Okay, yes, those are very…very *strange* coincidences, I'll give you that.

YOUNG MAN: Thank you.

YOUNG WOMAN: But where exactly do *I* come in here?

YOUNG MAN: *Right.* Yes. Well, after she told me things would happen in March and June, she told me that sometime after *that…* (*Smiles*) I'd meet the woman I'd spend the rest of my life with.

YOUNG WOMAN: And…did she say how you would actually *know* this?

YOUNG MAN: She said that I'd be in a place I go to all the time, which I do, and I'd see you.

YOUNG WOMAN: …That's it?

YOUNG MAN: Yeah. I mean, *no*. She described *you*! Like, *exactly* what you look like, I mean… (*Laughs*) *Wow*!

YOUNG WOMAN: A lot of people look like me. I don't exactly have an uncommon look.

YOUNG MAN: Right, but it's like you were pulled straight from my head, I mean… (*Laughs*) You're *exactly* what I pictured when she described you, it's crazy!

YOUNG WOMAN: I don't know. This seems like a bit of a stretch.

YOUNG MAN: (*Notices green juice*) *Oh*! *Oh*! I totally forgot the craziest part! She said she *also* saw us both partaking in *green*!

YOUNG WOMAN: "Partaking in green?"

YOUNG MAN: *Green*!

He holds up his green juice excitedly and points to her bowl of green food.

YOUNG MAN: *See*? *Green*!

YOUNG WOMAN: This whole place is people "partaking in green!" They've got *kale cookies*.

YOUNG MAN: But it's still possible! I mean, all the pieces fit!

YOUNG WOMAN: Let's just say she really *did* predict all this, okay? How do you know you coming up to me doesn't undo the whole thing?

YOUNG MAN: I thought about that too. But she said that some things, *big* things, are written in the stars. And the choices we make either get us there faster or slower.

YOUNG WOMAN: And I'm written in your stars…

YOUNG MAN: (*Smiling*) Yeah.

YOUNG WOMAN: …I wanna speak to this woman.

YOUNG MAN: What?

YOUNG WOMAN: (*Crosses arms*) Yeah. Face to face. That way I can see if she gets any *vibes* or whatever. I mean, if she's really all powerful in this kinda stuff I'm sure she'd be able to confirm whether or not I'm really this prophecy woman of yours.

YOUNG MAN: Well, she, um…she doesn't actually…live here.

YOUNG WOMAN: Okay, then where does she live?

YOUNG MAN: (*Sheepishly*) Um. Florida.

YOUNG WOMAN: *Florida*? You saw a psychic woman in Florida?

YOUNG MAN: *Yeah*, but—

YOUNG WOMAN: What the hell made you think that was a good idea?!

YOUNG MAN: I always promised my brother I'd fly down there whenever my nephew was born. And while I was there, my family convinced me to see a psychic!

YOUNG WOMAN: …You flew down to Florida just to see your newborn nephew?

YOUNG MAN: I mean…yeah.

YOUNG MAN: (*Begrudgingly*) …Fuck, that's cute.

YOUNG MAN: (*Smiling*) Yeah?

YOUNG WOMAN: But still, *Florida*?!

YOUNG MAN: I know! I know! But she couldn't have been *that* bad, right? I mean, everything she said is coming true!

YOUNG WOMAN: Okay, I think you're forgetting a very important factor in all this.

YOUNG MAN: What?

YOUNG WOMAN: What about me?

YOUNG MAN: Whaddya mean?

YOUNG WOMAN: Don't *I* have a say in all this? I mean, you keep saying all this was predicted and written in the stars and all that crap, but don't *I* get a choice in the matter? I mean, what if I don't want to be with someone for the rest of my life? Hm? What if you're not my type? And let's just say for a second I believe all this stuff. How do you know *my* stars don't say something different than *yours*? You ever think of that? And, *I'm sorry*, but after this psychic lady told you all this, did you really think going up to this person you thought was "the one" and *steamrolling* them with all this information was going to just sweep them off their feet? 'Cause I'll tell ya what! It doesn't! It's actually kinda freaky! And for all I know, I could be the fifteenth person you've approached in a place you go to, with something *green*, and who kinda looks like me! I don't know! But I do know that as cute as this may be in theory, it's all just a little much for me right now, so…I'm sorry about your job and your appendix, but I really think it'd be best if you just go and let me finish my lunch in peace. Okay? I just…*yeah*, I really think that'd be best.

Silence. YOUNG WOMAN pokes at the contents of her bowl with her fork, not looking up. YOUNG MAN, hurt, nods slowly, turns, and walks away. He stops and turns around.

YOUNG MAN: Look…if I'm being honest…I've spent my whole life trying to get things right. Maybe it's a fear of failure or something. But whatever I did…I always made sure I did it *right*. And maybe when she told me all those things, that's exactly what I started doing. Maybe I just fell right back into that pattern, I don't know. But as far as meeting "the one" goes…I've been in a lot of relationships that felt like I had already found that person. They really did. But they still ended. No matter what I did "right." So, when she told me that I was finally going to meet the one? Like, *the* one? I was over the moon, ya know? And even though I'd do anything to make this all fit and line up…I can't deny how I *felt* when I saw you just now. I mean, I literally gasped. You know how people do that in movies and stuff? Like… (*Gasps*) I did that. So it's not like I saw you and thought of all the details she told me and said, "*Yup*! This all fits!" Not at all. In fact…I know this is a really heavy thing to say, but…I knew I wanted to be with you before I even remembered there was a psychic. Then, when I started to realize all the pieces lined up, I just got so damn *excited* that I needed to come over and tell you! But…I shouldn't have bombarded you like this. I just…I wish I'd kept my big mouth shut and said hi. But, hey, at least getting it right wasn't the first thing on my mind, right? So…progress. (*Beat*) So, um… yeah, anyway, I just want to say… (*Into her eyes*) It was *really* nice meeting you. (*Beat*) Enjoy your lunch and, uh…have a good one.

Hesitantly, YOUNG MAN turns and walks away. He's almost gone when:

YOUNG WOMAN: …You should've led with that.

YOUNG MAN stops and turns back.

YOUNG MAN: What?
YOUNG WOMAN: The whole "doing the right thing" speech. You should've led with that.
YOUNG MAN: …I should've?
YOUNG WOMAN: What, you think "a psychic said you were my soulmate" was better?
YOUNG MAN: No, I guess not.

They stare at each other, both holding back a smile.

YOUNG WOMAN: …You wanna sit down?
YOUNG MAN: (*Nodding*) …Yeah. I do.

They smile fully at each other. YOUNG WOMAN motions for him to sit down.

YOUNG MAN: Right!

He sits across from her. They look at each other for a few moments.

YOUNG WOMAN: So…you got any pictures of this nephew?
YOUNG MAN: God, *so* many.

YOUNG MAN pulls out his phone, clicks around a few times and hands YOUNG WOMAN the phone. She scrolls through.

YOUNG WOMAN: Oh my *God*!
YOUNG MAN: I know, right?
YOUNG WOMAN: Look at him!

YOUNG WOMAN smiles at the photos for a few moments as YOUNG MAN watches her.

YOUNG WOMAN: So beautiful.
YOUNG MAN: (*Still looking at her*) Yeah.

YOUNG WOMAN looks up at him. They smile.

BLACKOUT.

END OF PLAY.

Toxic Norse-culinity

• • •

Production History

Toxic Norse-culinity was first performed at the Chain Theater in June 2021 for its Summer One Act Festival. It was directed by David Zayas, Jr.

SVEN: Alex Staub
BRETL: Andrew Goebel
KEVIN: Kirk Koczanowski

Special thanks to Joshua Mitchell for stepping into the role of SVEN for an encore presentation, learning the entire play and memorizing it in under forty-eight hours.

Toxic Norse-culinity was later performed in August 2022 for the Samuel French 47th Annual Off-Off-Broadway Festival. It was directed by David Zayas, Jr.

CHARACTERS

SVEN: A large Viking, recently back from raiding a foreign land.
BRETL: A tall, wiry Viking who has exiled himself from the village. Lives on the mountainside.
KEVIN: A modern guy in modern clothes. Dirty with hands tied.

SETTING
The side of a mountain overlooking a beautiful view.

NOTES
A "/" indicates when the next character begins their line.

High up on the plains of a mountainside. Harsh lands with rocks and howling winds. Ravens squawk in the distance. A hut sits Stage Left. SVEN, a large Viking, cloaked in furs, heavy boots, and a small axe on his belt enters Stage Right. He stops when he sees the hut. Nervous, he attempts to silently encourage himself, eventually closing his eyes and taking a deep breath. He laughs loudly as he strides forward, attempting to look as confident as possible.

SVEN: *Bretl*! Bretl, my friend, come out! I know you're in there, you landlocked fool!

BRETL, a wiry, though still menacing Viking, pokes his head out through the flaps of the hut. SVEN smiles with open arms.

SVEN: *Bretl*!

BRETL'S face morphs into a scowl.

SVEN: By the Gods, I almost thought I had wasted a journey! It has been a long time!

Awkward silence.

SVEN: Would you…would you not agree?

BRETL stares at SVEN. He disappears into the hut and comes back out moments later with an axe, ready to use it.

SVEN: Oh, so this is how you greet an old friend then, is it?

BRETL: *Friend*? Pah! You have some large balls to come here and call yourself my friend.

SVEN: *Aye.* Aye, I *do*! I *do* have large balls! Thank you for saying so!

BRETL: You do not! They are tiny! You are a coward and have coward's balls!

SVEN: They are enormous balls! Bigger than Thor's! Unlike *your* balls!

BRETL takes a few giant steps toward SVEN, who takes out his axe and braces himself.

BRETL: What was that? Did you insult my balls, coward?

SVEN: Perhaps! And I am not a coward and you know it!

BRETL: What I *know* is that I told you the next time I laid eyes upon you, I would bury my axe in your skull!

SVEN: Well, go on, then! *Try*! By the Gods, I *dare* you!

A tense standoff. BRETL puts his axe away.

BRETL: Pah. You are not worth the blood on my axe. Now get out of my sight before I change my mind.

BRETL walks toward the hut.

SVEN: I do not suppose you want to hear of my raids on the new lands we discovered, then?

BRETL: Eat a raven's arse, Sven.

SVEN: I will not!

BRETL: You will.

SVEN: I will *not*!

BRETL disappears into the hut.

SVEN: (*Calling out*) Then I will not be telling you of all the *treasure* I brought back! Treasure enough to fill the great hall of Asgard!

BRETL pokes his head out of the hut.

BRETL: ...You lie.
SVEN: (*Raises hand*) Hand to Odin.

BRETL studies SVEN, unsure.

BRETL: Your words are meaningless and I do not believe you for a second.
SVEN: You do not *have* to believe me because it is true! Besides, the treasure and riches were not even our greatest prize.
BRETL: Hah! Are you *drunk*? What could *possibly* be better than treasure?
SVEN: Not *what*, Bretl. *Who*.

SVEN goes to the edge of the stage and whistles.

KEVIN enters in torn jean shorts, a dirty, yet modern T-shirt, and filthy sneakers. His wrists are bound together with rope.

KEVIN: (*Looking offstage*) Are you guys seeing this freakin' view right now?! It's *beautiful*, man! It's like one of those pictures you'd get as your desktop background or one of those fancy framed pictures from IKEA. Ya know, the ones that don't *look* like they could be real, but I mean, *there it is*, right? I'm looking at it! (*Noticing BRETL*) Oh. Hey, man. What's up?

SVEN slowly turns to BRETL, proud of himself. BRETL looks at KEVIN, confused.

KEVIN: You guys okay over here? I heard a lot of yelling about balls and stuff.

BRETL: *This* is what is better than treasure? Someone who speaks in riddles and is soft like a child?

KEVIN: Whoa.

SVEN: He is not strong, no, but he is filled with knowledge and is infinitely wise!

BRETL: (*Rolls eyes*) *Wise*. Pah.

SVEN: *Yes! Wise!*

BRETL: And what wisdom does he possess that our village seer does not, hm?

SVEN: It is not the future he speaks of, it is the present! Of who we are *now* and how to better ourselves! After our raids, we took him captive, thinking he would work the land or the stables, the usual slave duties. But on the journey back, he began talking to the men about their lives, their ambitions, their... (*To KEVIN*) What is that word you use?

KEVIN: Feelings.

SVEN: *Feelings! Yes!* (*To BRETL*) At first, we thought it was madness! But some men took interest and began doing what he suggested. Eventually, the whole *ship* started listening! And ever since we arrived back, I have seen it spread throughout the entire village and I have watched all the men change! They have become *better*!

BRETL: Better? Better *how*?

SVEN: Just…*better*!

BRETL: At fighting? Sailing ships?

SVEN: In a way, yes! But all of those changes happened because *he* showed them how to be better men!

BRETL: "Better men?" What is this talk? We *fight*, we *raid*, and we *drink*. How else are you to be a "better man" than that?

SVEN: Well…uh…

KEVIN: (*To BRETL*) I got this. (*Stepping forward*) *Hi*. Bretl, right? Yeah, hi, I'm Kevin. Nice to meet you. (*Holds out hand*) No? Okay, all good. Look, I don't mean to interrupt or anything, but I just wanted to say that I've been captive for a few weeks now and have gotten to know you guys pretty well over that time and, yeah, those three things you just mentioned? The fighting, raiding, and drinking? Well, let me assure you, you're all *very* good at them. No doubt. Top notch, really. *But*…what Sven here is saying is that, what *I'm* doing is showing these guys that those three things? They don't necessarily *define* who you are as a man.

BRETL: Of *course* they do.

KEVIN: *Right. Okay. Well*…what *I'm* saying is *maaaaybe*…they *don't*. Eh? Maybe you can do whatever you wanna do as long as it makes you happy. Maybe there are other things besides those three that you like to do that might not be considered "manly" and that's okay!

BRETL: "Other things?" What "other things?"

KEVIN: Like…I don't know…weaving fabrics, picking flowers, spending time at home with the kids. Stuff like that.

BRETL: Women things?

KEVIN: *Ah*, see? Okay! Now let's talk about that comment for a second. See, those may be things that are typically *done* by women, right? But what if I were to tell you that there's nothing wrong with a *man* doing them?

BRETL: I would say you are mad.

KEVIN: Huh. Interesting. 'Cause I've seen women doing all the things you say make a *man*.

BRETL: What?

SVEN: He speaks of our shield-maidens.

KEVIN: Shield-maidens! Right! *Also* frightening. You let *them* do "man things," but it's not okay for men to do what you call "women things"? *Guys.* What's wrong with men getting in touch with their feminine side a little bit, huh?

KEVIN smiles, not expecting an answer.

SVEN: …Nothing?

KEVIN: *Exactly*! *Nothing*! You both can do any of those things as long as it makes you happy, and it doesn't make you any less of a man! (*Smiling*) Whoa! Look at you, big guy! Good job, Sven.

SVEN grins, proud. BRETL looks between SVEN and KEVIN, confused.

BRETL: (*Suddenly angry*) Enough of this! I will not listen to any more of this childish talk!

SVEN: It is not childish! It is wise! It has made the men become less cruel and more understanding! It is truly a sight, Bretl!

BRETL: We are *Vikings*, you *dung beetle*! We are *supposed* to be cruel! But here you stand telling me that this *slave* has changed our people's very nature and it does not bother you? Sounds to me like he is a trickster trying to weaken us! Perhaps he is even Loki in disguise, tricking your minds and hearts to make the men of Odin soft and weak for the great battle to come at Ragnarok! Did you not think of that?!

SVEN: He is not *Loki*! He is Kevin. And he has helped the entire village grow and work together! But you would not know that because you hide up here on your little mountain and *never* come to the village!

BRETL: And why would I come to the village when *you* are there? After I swore to never see your pig face ever again.

SVEN: Pig face? *You* have a pig face!

BRETL: I do not. *You* are the one with a pig face.

SVEN: At least *I'm* not a goat kisser!

BRETL takes his axe out.

BRETL: *That was only once!*

KEVIN jumps in the middle of them.

KEVIN: *Whoa-whoa-whoa.* Hey! Guys! Chill for a second, okay?! *Chill!*

BRETL and SVEN stare each other down.

KEVIN: *Geez.* You people go from zero to murder in, like, a *second* around here. (*To SVEN*) I'm confused, I thought you said you two were friends.

SVEN: Apparently I was mistaken.

BRETL: *Oh*, that you were! You *were* mistaken! After what you pulled.

SVEN: Come now, *this* again?

BRETL: *Aye*! *This* again!

KEVIN: (*To SVEN*) What's he talking about?

SVEN: Nothing. It was nothing.

BRETL: "*Nothing*?" Ooh, I really *should* bury this axe in your skull!

SVEN: Go ahead and try!

KEVIN: Whoa, hey, *guys*! Come on, let's just…talk this out, okay? Can we do that? Can we talk it out?

SVEN and BRETL don't say anything but instead look away, grumpily.

KEVIN: Okay. Good. *Now*. Bretl. You're clearly very upset with Sven about something, right? You wanna tell me what that something is?

BRETL: …He betrayed me.

SVEN: Oh, I did not *betray/you*!

BRETL: You *did*!

SVEN: I did *not*!

KEVIN: *Ah-ah-ah*! Okay, alright, let's just…pause right here for a second, okay? We're pausing. Sven, c'mere.

KEVIN and SVEN take a few steps away from BRETL, who is confused.

KEVIN: *Sveeen.* What's up, man? You've come a really long way these last few weeks, but the second we get up here you start acting like the *old* you! *Balls* this, *balls* that. So many balls, Sven! Come on. You don't wanna go *backward* now, do you?

SVEN: (*Sheepishly*) …I do not.

KEVIN: Okay! Good, that's what I wanna hear! Now, I want you to say the motto I taught you.

SVEN: (*Sheepishly*) …I do not want to say.

KEVIN: *Come oooon.* You said you wanted me here because you might need my help and guidance, so here it is! So, come on. I wanna hear it!

SVEN peaks at BRETL, embarrassed. He leans closer to KEVIN.

SVEN: I will be respectful of others and what they have to say…

KEVIN: *Aaand?*

SVEN: And…I will not lash out if I do not like their words.

KEVIN: That's *right*! See? You know this! So, let's go back there and make some real progress, okay?

SVEN: (*Sheepishly*) …Okay.

KEVIN: Great. And remember…you can do this! Right?

SVEN nods taking a deep breath.

KEVIN: (*Smiling*) Alright.

KEVIN and SVEN go back to BRETL who does not understand what has just happened.

KEVIN: Now, Sven. Bretl here seems to think you betrayed him in some way or another. Is there any reason he may think that?
SVEN: …Nay.

BRETL starts to speak. KEVIN holds up a hand to BRETL to stop him, though both hands go up because they are bound. KEVIN turns to SVEN, leans in, and gives him a look. SVEN shuffles his feet and looks at the ground.

SVEN: Perhaps. (*Begrudgingly*) Our village hosts a large festival to the Gods every hundredth moon cycle. Only a select few are chosen by the village elders to attend. It is a great honor to be chosen, and *I* had the honor of being picked.
KEVIN: Hey, that's great!
SVEN: Aye. I agree. (*Remembers*) Thank you. *So*, after all of the participants were chosen, the elders told us we were allowed to bring someone with us to the festival. And I asked Bretl if he cared to be my guest.
KEVIN: Aw, that's so nice.
SVEN: *But*…I was not truly *bringing* Bretl as my guest…I was bringing him…as…a, um…a…
KEVIN: As a what?
SVEN: Uh…
BRETL: *A sacrifice*! He brought me to the festival as a sacrifice! *Without telling me*!

Embarrassed, SVEN looks at KEVIN, who looks disappointed.

KEVIN: *Sveeeen.*
SVEN: *I know*! I know!
KEVIN: That's not something we *doooo.*
SVEN: It was not honorable and I admit that I should not have been deceptive!
BRETL: *Deceptive*?!/Pah!
KEVIN: No, you shouldn't have.
SVEN: But I did not do it to be *cruel*! I *swear* it!
BRETL: How is sacrificing me to the Gods without my knowledge *not* cruel? *Hm*?!
SVEN: That's...I...

KEVIN opens his mouth to speak, but BRETL steps forward, holding up his hand

BRETL: *Nay-nay-nay-nay*! I want you to tell me! I want you to tell me right here and now what on Midgard made you believe doing that was anything other than a low, cruel, and Helheim-worthy betrayal, Sven! *Go on*! I want you to finally tell me after all this time!
SVEN: I...I...

Struggling, SVEN looks at KEVIN for help. KEVIN waits for SVEN to produce an answer, attempting to look encouraging. SVEN looks back at BRETL. SVEN deflates.

BRETL: You are a *coward* and a *betrayer*. And you have wasted enough of my time. Now take your useless slave and be gone from here. I never want to see your face around here again.

BRETL turns and walks toward his hut.

SVEN: *You were the only one who was worthy!*

BRETL stops and turns around.

BRETL: …What?
SVEN: You were the only one…who was worthy. There was no one else I wished to bring.
BRETL: I…do not understand.
KEVIN: Me neither.
SVEN: When I was chosen for the festival, the elders told us of all the wonderful things the festival would hold for us. All the pleasures and joys we would experience. But they told us that the greatest reward was not for us…but for someone else. For the person we cared about most deeply. The elders were to perform a ritual which would open one of the many doors to Valhalla itself! And whomever we brought would be sacrificed and given the gift of endless riches and forever dining with the Gods! They gave us one hour to decide, but I knew immediately it was you. I thought, "Bretl has been my best friend since we were boys! He's been my greatest ally on the battlefield! There is no other person who I would want to have this reward than my best friend, Bretl!" But every time I went to tell you, I felt so uncertain! Uncertain that you would feel the same about our friendship and laugh in

my face! I worried you only thought of me as just another man in the shield wall. So...the moons came and went, and I never found the courage to tell you. The next thing I knew, we were standing at the ritual and you were staring at me with all of Helheim in your eyes. And before I could explain, you began to fight your way out of the festival, and I never forgave myself. *Never.* Now, was it honorable to bring you as a sacrifice without your knowledge? *Nay.* It was *not.* And if given the chance, I would go back and change my actions. But I cannot. I cannot change them. But I will tell you this, my friend. If I could, I'd go back a thousand times and always choose you as my sacrifice. Because you will always be the greatest thing in my life. *That* I am sure of.

KEVIN puts both of his palms together and places his hands on his mouth, nodding with tears of joy. BRETL looks around confused and begins rubbing his chest.

BRETL: What is this...what is this...*feeling* inside of my chest? Like warm ale coursing through my body on a winter's day.
KEVIN: That's *love*, Bretl. *Love.*

BRETL rubs his chest and arms in discomfort.

SVEN: Bretl, I am sorry for betraying you and for offering you as a sacrifice without your knowledge. My intentions were pure, but I was a fool in my actions. I hope that one day... you can forgive me.
BRETL: (*Uncomfortable*) I...I...

Fighting the feeling, BRETL takes out his axe and pulls it back as if to attack. SVEN doesn't move. As quickly as the axe goes up, BRETL deflates, full of love and emotion.

BRETL: I *do*. I *do* forgive you.
SVEN: …You do?
BRETL: Aye. And perhaps it is *I* who should be sorry. I was often angry and distant and should have shown you that I always thought of you as a true friend as well. Nay…a *brother*.
SVEN: (*Getting choked up*) A…a *brother*?
BRETL: Aye. A brother. Will you forgive *me*?
SVEN: Of…of *course*, Bretl. Of course.

SVEN and BRETL stare at each other, both on the verge of tears. KEVIN leans over to SVEN.

KEVIN: (*Whispers*) Go to him.

Immediately, SVEN and BRETL meet in the middle of the stage, giving each other the biggest of hugs, full of love, compassion, and happy cries. KEVIN watches, happily. He sighs with a shake of his head and a huge smile on his face.

KEVIN: Now *that's* a beautiful view. (*Calls out*) You two take your time, okay? I'll be over here if you need me. (*To self*) Ya did it again, Kevin. Ya did it again.

KEVIN exits from where he came, staring off at the view as he does.

SVEN and BRETL separate but stay close. They look off at where KEVIN exited.

BRETL: You were right about that one. He truly *is* remarkable.
SVEN: (*Smiling*) That he is.
BRETL: What did you say the land you raided was called?
SVEN: Brooklyn.
BRETL: Ah. Brooklyn.

BLACKOUT.

END OF PLAY.

Who You Are to Me

● ● ●

CHARACTERS

CARA: Early 30s.
GRACE: Early teens.

SETTING
A decent-sized apartment during a rainstorm.

NOTES
A "/" indicates when the next character begins their line.

Heavy rain pelts the windows of a decent-sized apartment. Only the light of a TV illuminates the living room. On the couch, CARA, early thirties, lies on her side, balled up under a blanket in matching pajamas. She has been crying. On a side table next to the couch sits a pile of crumpled-up tissues and a cup of tea.

The Princess Bride *plays on the TV. CARA watches, sniffling several times and wiping her face with a tissue. She makes sad noises during the dialogue. When the main character whispers, "As you wish," CARA cries harder.*

A loud, hurried knock on the front door. CARA sits up. She looks at the time on her phone, charging on the side table. Another knock, longer this time. CARA turns on a light and pauses the TV. She stares at the door, unsure.

GRACE: (*Offstage*) *Cara?* It's *Grace!* You *home?*
CARA: (*To herself*) *Grace?*
GRACE: Please be home…

Another knock. CARA opens the door. GRACE, early teens, stands in the doorway, soaking wet.

CARA: *Grace?!*
GRACE: Oh, thank God.

GRACE bursts passed CARA into the living room. CARA closes the door.

CARA: What're you doing here? Is everything/alright?

GRACE: Don't be mad, okay? I just needed to see you and it couldn't wait.

CARA: I'm not mad, I'm just—(*Re: GRACE'S clothes*) Were you out in this?

GRACE: Well, yeah, but only 'cause my phone died on the bus, so I couldn't call you or get an Uber, so I had to walk here.

CARA: You walked in this from the *bus stop*?! That's over a mile away!

GRACE: I mean, I know that *now*!

CARA: Grace, you know you're not supposed to be out this late—

GRACE: I *know*!

CARA: Let alone take the bus—

GRACE: I *know*, okay? But I had to see you!

CARA: (*Struggling*) ...*Okay*, but—

GRACE: You've *gotta* take Bryant back.

CARA: (*Taken aback*) ...What? How do/you—

GRACE: Bryant told my dad and me yesterday that he needed to stay with us 'cause you guys had a broken water pipe or something, and you guys weren't allowed in the apartment. So, I was like, "Well, why isn't *Cara* here then?" And he was like, "Oh, well, she wanted to stay with *her* family." Which didn't make any sense 'cause I know your parents live like two hours away, right? So, I called him out on it at dinner tonight, and he admitted the *real* reason he's staying with us is because you two broke up. And I know you two've had big fights before, but you've never broken up, so whatever stupid thing he did, which I'm *sure* was really stupid, you've *gotta* forgive him and you've *gotta* take him back. (*Remembering*) Please.

CARA stares at GRACE.

CARA: (*Taking a breath*) ...I'll get you a towel.

CARA exits to the other room.

CARA: (*Offstage*) And don't sit on anything!
GRACE: *Okay!*

GRACE looks around. She rubs the cold from her arms. CARA enters with a towel and some folded clothes.

CARA: Here.
GRACE: *Yes.* Your PJs are the best.
CARA: These are your brother's.
GRACE: *What?* Where are the ones you got for Christmas, like, four years ago?
CARA: They're dirty.
GRACE: Pajamas can't get dirty. They're *pajamas.*

CARA extends the clothes out to her.

GRACE: (*Rolling eyes*) Fine.

GRACE takes the clothes and towel and exits to the bathroom.

CARA: And don't leave your wet clothes on the floor please! Hang them up in the shower.
GRACE: *Okay!*
CARA: And if you want me to charge your phone—

GRACE'S arm appears from the doorway, holding her phone. CARA takes it. She goes to the side table, unplugs her phone, and plugs in GRACE'S. CARA stands up tall, closes her eye, takes a deep breath. Throughout the next lines, CARA goes to the kitchen, takes out a mug, puts in a teabag, and pours in hot water. She brings the mug to the couch.

CARA: (*Calling out*) I assume Bryant and your dad don't know you're here?

GRACE: (*Offstage*) They think I'm asleep. They're watching that boring Tom Hanks movie that came out this year and those are usually really long, so I figured I've got at least three hours before they check on me.

CARA: Assuming they don't fall asleep.

GRACE: *I know!* And *girls* get the bad rap for falling asleep during movies! (*Beat*) Oh, come—*Seriously*?

CARA: What?

GRACE exits the bathroom in matching pajamas patterned with obnoxiously large comic book characters.

GRACE: (*Unamused*) Why is my brother *seriously* a twelve-year-old...

CARA: (*Smiling lightly*) I made you some tea.

GRACE: Oh, awesome.

They both sit on the couch. GRACE picks up the tea. She notices the paused movie.

GRACE: Oh, man, *The Princess Bride*?!

CARA: Oh. Yeah.

GRACE: I *love* this movie! I haven't watched it in, like, forever! Since you babysat me, I think.

CARA: Only way I could get you to sit still.

GRACE: I remember I was watching it the night Bryant came home from college. Then *you* came out of the kitchen and he was all like—(*Wide-eyed*) "Who're *you*?"

GRACE laughs.

CARA: (*Smiles sadly*) …Yeah.

GRACE'S smile fades. Awkward silence. They drink their tea.

GRACE: Thanks. For the tea, I mean. It's really good.

CARA: You're welcome.

GRACE: And for the PJs. They're not so bad.

Silence.

CARA: So, uh…did Bryant explain to you…why we're…

GRACE: *No.* I tried asking, but he just got all mopey and stuff. Then my dad yelled at me 'cause I kept saying he probably did something *stupid.*

CARA: Why do you assume he did something stupid?

GRACE: He's a boy. They *always* do something stupid.

CARA: That's…usually true. But not this time.

GRACE: Then what? Did *you* do something stupid?

CARA: No, no one did anything.

GRACE: Then why break up?

CARA: It's hard to explain.

GRACE: (*Annoyed*) Why? 'Cause you think I won't get it?

CARA: No, I know you'd get it. It's just not an easy answer.

GRACE: Try anyway.

CARA: (*Sighs*) We... (*Beat*) Grew apart.

GRACE: ...Grew apart.

CARA: Yeah.

GRACE: You just...grew apart.

CARA: Yes.

GRACE: ...That's *stupid*. I don't believe that for, like, a *second*.

CARA: Well, it's true.

GRACE: What does that even mean? "Grew apart?"

CARA: It means, that even when you're dating someone or you're married, you still grow as people. And sometimes who you grow into doesn't always work with the person you're with.

GRACE: But you two've been together for, like, *ever*! You're saying you just *randomly* grew apart?

CARA: No, it's been happening for a while.

GRACE: *When*? You two were fine the last couple of times I saw you!

CARA: We were putting on a good face for you and your dad.

GRACE: That's so stupid.

CARA: I know it might not make sense—

GRACE: I didn't say it didn't make any sense, I just said it was stupid.

CARA: ...Fair enough.

GRACE: (*Realizes*) So...wait, is that, like, the *only* reason you two are breaking up?

CARA: Well, it's...not exactly a small thing, but...yes.

GRACE: Then, this is, like, *totally* easy! All we've gotta do is figure out how to make you two grow back together and you'll be fine!

CARA: It doesn't work like that.

GRACE: Sure it does! If you grew apart, you can grow *back*! We just gotta find something that does that!

CARA: We've been trying to do that, Grace. For the last year or so.

GRACE: Like what? What have you tried?

CARA: Everything.

GRACE: Well, obviously not! You're breaking up!

CARA: I promise you, if there was something that could fix this, we would've done it.

GRACE: So what? You're just gonna *give up*?

CARA: This wasn't an easy decision for us, Grace! It's probably the hardest thing we've ever done!

GRACE: (*Remembering*) *Oh*! There was this article! I was reading it on the way here before my phone died and it listed, like, fifteen things people can do to save their relationship! Maybe one of those will help!

CARA: I really doubt it, Grace.

GRACE: You never know! If my phone's back on, I'll show you!

GRACE stands.

CARA: (*Stopping her*) I don't wanna see it. Okay?

GRACE: Why not? It could help!

CARA: (*Exhausted*) I really don't think it will.

GRACE stares at CARA, confused. Anger bubbling up.

GRACE: Why are you so *okay* with this?!

CARA: What're you talking about?

GRACE: You're, like, not even upset at *all*!

CARA: Of *course* I'm upset, Grace. I'm barely holding it together here.

GRACE: You seem *fine* to me!

CARA: Just because I'm not crying my eyes out right now doesn't mean I don't *want* to.

GRACE: Well, maybe you *should*! It'd show you actually *care*!

CARA: Of *course* I care! That's why this is so damn hard for me!

GRACE: *No*! No, it *isn't*! It isn't hard at *all*! You're probably *happy* this is happening!

CARA: What? Why would I/be—

GRACE: 'Cause now you won't have to deal with me or my stupid family ever again! You get to find someone *new* and marry *him* and spend all your time with *his* family and love *them* more than *us*! (*Tearing up*) You'll become best friends with *his* little sister and you'll pick *her* up from school and ask her all about *her* life and boys and grades and help her with *her* math homework and make dinner with *her* and I won't even pop into your head because you moved on and forgot I ever existed!

GRACE falls back onto the couch and covers her face. She sobs. CARA deflates. She understands now. Silence.

CARA: Grace…

CARA puts a hand on GRACE, who pulls away.

CARA: (*Gently*) Grace, come on. Look at me.
GRACE: (*Into hands*) No.
CARA: Please? *Please* look at me?

GRACE drops her hands. Hesitantly, she looks at CARA.

CARA: That's not going to happen, okay? I promise.
GRACE: (*Voice shaking*) How do you know?
CARA: Because I would never let it.
GRACE: Yeah, but, like…how do you *know*, though? How do you know we won't just become *strangers*?

They stare at each other. CARA searches for the right words. Her walls slowly crumble. Tears build in her eyes. She tries to smile through, but the tears come anyway.

CARA: (*Through tears*) I don't know, Grace. I really don't. But I *do* know that the possibility of not having you in my life has been one of the hardest parts of this whole thing. 'Cause it's always been you and me. Right? Even before Bryant, it's always been you and me. And I don't want that to change. It can't. Because seeing how strong and smart and confident you are makes *me* want to be those things. And I need that. Besides, no one else knows how to make me laugh like you. Or knows when I need them to be brutally honest and when to lie to me. You've never just been my boyfriend's little sister, Grace. Or some kid I used to babysit. (*Getting choked up*) You're the sister I never had. And the thought of not having you in my life kills me. It *kills* me. So…no…I don't know whether or not we'll become strangers. But I *do* know that

I'm going to do everything to make sure that never happens. Not just for you but for *me*. I *promise*. Okay?

GRACE quickly goes to CARA and hugs her.

GRACE: (*Half-crying*) Okay.

They hold each other for a long while. They separate. They smile at each other.

CARA: (*Points to face*) Is my face a mess?
GRACE: Always.

They laugh. CARA grabs tissues. Hands some to GRACE.

GRACE: Thanks.

They wipe their noses and compose themselves.

CARA: I should get you home, soon.
GRACE: You think I can stay here tonight?
CARA: Only if you call your dad and let him know you snuck out.
GRACE: …Maybe just another hour then.
CARA: (*Laughs lightly*) Okay.
GRACE: (*Re: paused TV*) Can we watch a little?
CARA: (*Smiling*) Yeah. Sure.

CARA picks up the remote. They both adjust themselves.

CARA: Ready?
GRACE: Wait.

GRACE grabs a pillow, puts it on CARA'S lap, and lies down with her head on the pillow.

GRACE: Ready.

CARA stares at GRACE. She smiles. CARA clicks the remote, the movie turns back on. They both watch. CARA begins to play with GRACE'S hair as the lights slowly fade and only the light of the TV illuminates them.

BLACKOUT.

END OF PLAY.

3 Characters Figure It Out

• • •

Production History

3 Characters Figure It Out was first performed at the Chain Theater in January 2022 for its Winter One Act Festival. It was directed by David Zayas, Jr.

STAGE DIRECTIONS: Caroline Orlando
CHARACTER 1: Sunita Deshpande
CHARACTER 2: Carlos Joy
CHARACTER 3: Kirk Koczanowski

CHARACTERS

STAGE DIRECTIONS: Any age. Any gender.
CHARACTER 1: Any age. Any gender.
CHARACTER 2: Any age. Any gender.
CHARACTER 3: Any age. Any gender.

NOTES
A "/" indicates when the next character begins their line.

Lights up to half. CHARACTERS 1, 2, and 3 stand in the half light, waiting as patiently as each character can as STAGE DIRECTIONS stands Downstage Left in a bright light, smiling, happy to be there. STAGE DIRECTIONS casually waves and points at members of the audience as if to say, "Hi!" and "I see you!" This goes on for some time. Eventually, CHARACTERS 1, 2, and 3 look at each other confused and unsure of what to do. With no warning and perhaps in the middle of waving and saying hello to people, STAGE DIRECTIONS speaks.

STAGE DIRECTIONS: Lights up!

Lights shoot up. CHARACTERS 1, 2, and 3 recoil from the bright light.

CHARACTER 1: (*Simultaneous*) Whoa.
CHARACTER 2: (*Simultaneous*) Jesus Christ.
CHARACTER 3: (*Simultaneous*) *Ah*, that's…okay.

STAGE DIRECTIONS smiles as the three CHARACTERS' eyes adjust.

STAGE DIRECTIONS: Three characters stand onstage. Silence.

The three CHARACTERS stand, waiting. The moment gets longer and longer. They stare out at the audience, trying to wait patiently. After some time, they awkwardly glance at each other and then in the direction of STAGE DIRECTIONS, who still smiles. They look back at each other as if to say, "What do we do?" and "I don't know."

CHARACTER 3: (*To CHARACTER 1*) Should we...should we *do* something?

CHARACTER 1: We gotta wait until they say.

CHARACTER 3: Oh.

CHARACTER 2: (*Under breath*) This is so stupid.

Awkward silence. All the CHARACTERS look around, impatiently. STAGE DIRECTIONS smiles at the audience.

CHARACTER 3: Do we know what we're waiting/*for*?

STAGE DIRECTIONS: Lightning strikes!

Lightning crashes and thunder booms overhead. All CHARACTERS duck and recoil.

CHARACTER 1: (*Simultaneous*) *Geez*!

CHARACTER 2: (*Simultaneous*) *Holy* hell!

CHARACTER 3: (*Simultaneous*) *Ah*!

STAGE DIRECTIONS: The three characters look at the sky, concerned.

Unsure, all CHARACTERS look at each other and then at the sky, though all in different directions.

STAGE DIRECTIONS: They see a storm coming in the far distance.

CHARACTER 2: (*Pointing up*) But...wasn't it just—

STAGE DIRECTIONS: Fearful of the storm, Character 1 proclaims that they should begin their search before the storm arrives.

CHARACTER 1: (*Nodding*) *Right.* Okay. (*Proclaiming*) …
Oh, *look*! A *storm*! We should begin our search before the
storm arrives!

CHARACTER 3: What search?

CHARACTER 1: We don't know yet, just go with it.

STAGE DIRECTIONS: Character 2 *gleefully* expresses their
delight that the search has finally begun.

CHARACTER 2: (*Rolls eyes*) Jesus. (*Unenthusiastic*) Oh, how
great. The search has finally begun.

*STAGE DIRECTION'S smile becomes a bit forced. Silence.
CHARACTERS 1 and 3 look at CHARACTER 2. CHARACTER
2 notices.*

CHARACTER 2: *What?*

CHARACTER 3: I think you gotta…

CHARACTER 1: Yeah, you gotta do it *gleefully.*

CHARACTER 2: I *did.*

CHARACTER 3: Um.

CHARACTER 1: I think they want it to be more gleeful.

CHARACTER 2: *More* gleeful? I'm not doing it more gleeful! And what the hell kinda writing even *is* that anyway?
"*Gleefully?*"

CHARACTER 1: Hey, I'm not the one who makes this stuff/
up, alright?

CHARACTER 2: It's just so *stupid*! Why do we always/have
to do what they say?

CHARACTER 1: I *know* it is, but you just gotta do it, okay?
Just do it.

CHARACTER 2: *Fine.* (*Overly gleeful*) *Oooh*! How *grand*! The journey has *finally* begun!

CHARACTER 2 does a quick sarcastic dance. STAGE DIRECTIONS slowly turns to CHARACTER 2, who smiles at them. STAGE DIRECTIONS turns back around, annoyed. They shake it off before moving on with a smile.

STAGE DIRECTIONS: All three characters begin their search. They start walking in a giant circle around the stage.

Begrudgingly, all three CHARACTERS walk in a big circle around the stage.

STAGE DIRECTIONS: They continue to walk. Which eventually turns into a jog.

All three CHARACTERS sigh and start jogging together. They do this for a long while. They eventually start to feel the effects of the jog. STAGE DIRECTIONS continues to smile out to the audience, this time a bit smug.

STAGE DIRECTIONS: Faster.

All the CHARACTERS jog faster, slowly getting more and more winded, throwing aggravated glances at STAGE DIRECTIONS every time they jog by.

CHARACTER 3: How long is this gonna go on for?
CHARACTER 2: *Seriously.*

CHARACTER 1: I don't know.

CHARACTER 3: 'Cause I've got *asthma*! I don't know if they know that, but I do! Well, not *full* asthma but a version of it that could really mess me up if I keep—

STAGE DIRECTIONS: Character 1 stops, abruptly.

CHARACTER 1 stops, abruptly. The other two stop and look back.

CHARACTER 2: What's up?

CHARACTER 1: I stepped on something.

STAGE DIRECTIONS: Character 1 looks down at something under their right foot.

CHARACTER 1: (*Looking down*) Wait. Is that…(*Realizing*) Oh my God. Oh my *God*!

CHARACTER 3: What?

CHARACTER 1: (*To Stage Directions*) Are you kidding me right now?!

CHARACTER 3: What? What is it?

CHARACTER 2: What happened?

CHARACTER 1: (*Sighs*) …I stepped on a landmine.

CHARACTER 3: *What*?!

CHARACTER 1: Yeah.

CHARACTER 3: Are you freakin' *serio*—a *landmine*?!

CHARACTER 2: (*To Stage Directions*) What the hell's a matter with you?!

STAGE DIRECTIONS: *Hey*, you know how this works. I don't make this crap up. I just say what was written.

CHARACTER 2: Unbelievable.

CHARACTER 3: I knew this play was gonna be weird, but I didn't think it was gonna be *this* kinda play!

CHARACTER 2: And what kinda play is that exactly?

CHARACTER 3: I don't know! *Tension* and-and-and *explosives* and stuff!

CHARACTER 1: Look, I know this isn't ideal, but I think we're gonna be fine.

CHARACTER 3: How can you say that?! You're the one *standing* on the freakin' thing!

CHARACTER 1: *Yes*, but think about it. When's the last time you heard of someone blowing up onstage? Hm?

CHARACTER 3: (*Thinking*) …Um.

CHARACTER 2: Maybe this is, like, the playwright's *thing* or whatever.

CHARACTER 1: Whaddya mean?

CHARACTER 2: I don't know, playwrights nowadays like to do all sorts of crazy crap like that. "Push boundaries" or whatever. Makes 'em think they're *cool* or *edgy*, so…yeah. Maybe this is their thing.

CHARACTER 1: (*To Stage Directions*) Is it?

STAGE DIRECTIONS: (*Turning*) Is it what?

CHARACTER 1: Is this the playwright's *thing*? Blowing people up.

STAGE DIRECTIONS: *I* don't know.

CHARACTER 2: Whaddya mean you don't know?!

STAGE DIRECTIONS: I don't know the playwright *personally*, I just read what they wrote, okay?!

CHARACTER 2: (*High-pitched mocking*) "I just read what they wrote, okay?!" Well, I hope punching you in the neck is what's written next.

STAGE DIRECTIONS opens their mouth to say something, but CHARACTER 1 stops them.

CHARACTER 1: Alright, okay, let's just…

STAGE DIRECTIONS turns back around, peeved.

CHARACTER 3: (*Looking around*) Do you think there are *more* landmines?!

CHARACTER 1: I doubt it. This play's already too weird for *multiple* casualties. Even if blowing people up is their "thing," I'm sure the writer just wanted to raise the stakes or something.

CHARACTER 2: So the first thing they think of is a landmine?! Who the hell is this guy?

CHARACTER 3: How do you know it's a guy?

CHARACTER 2: What, you really think a *woman* would write something this stupid?

CHARACTER 3: *I* think a woman can do *anything*.

CHARACTER 2: Okay, I might not know what the hell this play is about, but I can assure you it's not that.

CHARACTER 1: Just…forget all that, alright? We gotta keep this thing going. Go see if there's something we can put on this to replace my foot.

CHARACTER 3: Like what?

CHARACTER 1: I don't know. A rock or something.

CHARACTER 2: A *rock*?

CHARACTER 1: *Just*…see what you can find!

CHARACTERS 2 and 3 look around the stage and maybe the audience.

CHARACTER 3: I don't see anything.
CHARACTER 2: Me neither.
CHARACTER 1: There's gotta be *something* around here.
CHARACTER 2: Nope. They gave us zero props.
CHARACTER 1: *What? Nothing?*
CHARACTER 2: Apparently our writer is a *minimalist* who enjoys explosive devices.
CHARACTER 3: (*Coming back*) It's true. There's nothing here, just us.

CHARACTER 1 closes their eyes and pinches the brim of their nose.

CHARACTER 1: Okay, just…let me think about this for a second. Um. So, *something* needs to happen for the play to continue, right? Something to keep it moving forward?
CHARACTER 3: Yeah.
CHARACTER 1: So if I'm stuck here with nothing to get me off of this thing, then…that means…something needs to come to *us*! Yeah! So, we just need to wait!
CHARACTER 3: You think we should just…wait?
CHARACTER 1: Until something happens, yeah.
CHARACTER 3: But, how do we know there even *is* something coming?
STAGE DIRECTIONS: (*Dramatically*) Out of the sky, an enormous dragon swoops in! Claws and legs swiping at the characters!

STAGE DIRECTIONS makes big swooping gestures and dragon noises. Silence. All the CHARACTERS turn and look at STAGE DIRECTIONS, who eventually notices. CHARACTER 2 shakes their head, angry.

STAGE DIRECTIONS: ...What?

CHARACTER 1: You're kidding, right?

STAGE DIRECTIONS: (*Proud*) Of course not.

CHARACTER 2: Look at this theater, ya idiot! You think they've got a budget for *dragon legs*?!

STAGE DIRECTIONS: That's not the playwright's problem! If they wanted to do this play, then it was up to the producers to *produce* what was written!

CHARACTER 2: Oh, so the playwright gets to put in whatever impossible shit they want and then just turn around and say, "Good luck, bitch!"

STAGE DIRECTIONS: Pretty much, yeah!

CHARACTER 2: Well, that's some lazy-ass writing.

CHARACTER 1: And rude.

CHARACTER 3: *Really* rude! To the theater and their budget!

STAGE DIRECTIONS: You all ever heard the phrase "don't shoot the messenger"?!

CHARACTER 2: Okay, don't get cute, dude.

CHARACTER 3: We're just trying to figure all this out!

STAGE DIRECTIONS: You don't *need* to figure it out! You just need to shut up and do what the play says! How about that?!

CHARACTER 1: *Hey-hey*! Let's just...calm down for a second, alright? *Chill*. Now, it's obvious they don't have dragon legs to use this time around, so maybe we can just...skip them.

Just this once. That way we can keep the play going and not have this one issue derail the whole thing. *Hm*? Can we do that?

STAGE DIRECTIONS: …Fine.

CHARACTER 1: Okay! Great! No dragon legs.

STAGE DIRECTIONS: *This* time.

CHARACTER 1: This time. Yes.

CHARACTER 3: Great!

CHARACTER 2: (*Flatly*) Yeah. Great.

CHARACTER 3: So…what happens next, then? (*Laughs nervously*) Can't be worse than *dragon legs*.

STAGE DIRECTIONS: (*Very serious*) Character 1 pulls out a gun.

All the CHARACTERS freeze. They slowly look at STAGE DIRECTIONS.

CHARACTER 2: You're an/*asshole*, dude.

CHARACTER 1: I'm/*sorry*?

CHARACTER 3: In *today's* world?! You really think it's a good idea to pull out/a *gun*?!

STAGE DIRECTIONS pulls out a gun and aims it at them.

STAGE DIRECTIONS: I said—

CHARACTER 1: (*Simultaneous*) *Whoa*!

CHARACTER 2: (*Simultaneous*) *Jesus Christ*!

CHARACTER 3: (*Simultaneous*) What the *heck*, man?!

CHARACTER 2: What the *hell's* the matter with you?! You just made the audience get all weird!

STAGE DIRECTIONS: *Look*! I don't make up the rules, okay?! I just follow them! Because that is my *job*! To tell you all what the hell is going on here and make sure what the playwright wrote is followed and respected! But you all keep farting around and doing your *own* damn thing, ruining the show, and it's driving me *nuts*! So if I've gotta make sure this thing continues to go smoothly, even if that means *forcing* you, *I'm going to*! Now, I *said, Character 1 pulls out a gun*!

CHARACTER 1: I don't *have* a gun! *You* do!

Awkward silence. Embarrassed, STAGE DIRECTIONS sheepishly walks over to CHARACTER 1 and hands them the gun, then goes back to their spot. CHARACTER 1 awkwardly holds the gun in the palms of their hands. All three CHARACTERS look at each other.

CHARACTER 1: *Great.* Thank you. Now, and I'm hesitant to even ask this, but what the hell happens *next*?

STAGE DIRECTIONS opens their mouth, stops, then looks confused.

STAGE DIRECTIONS: …Huh.

CHARACTER 3: What?

STAGE DIRECTIONS: That's…that's it.

CHARACTER 2: Whaddya mean, "That's it"?

STAGE DIRECTIONS: That's it! That's the end of the stage directions!

CHARACTER 2: *What*?

CHARACTER 1: Are you sure?

STAGE DIRECTIONS: Yes, that's all I have! It just…*ends.*

CHARACTER 3: (*Confused*) So…the play was just supposed to end with someone pulling out a gun?

STAGE DIRECTIONS: I guess.

Small silence.

CHARACTER 2: What kinda avant-garde bullshit *is this*?!

CHARACTER 1: So, wait, hold on…we're *beyond* the end of the play now?

STAGE DIRECTIONS: I…I don't know! I *guess* so!

CHARACTER 3: We're *beyond* the end?

CHARACTER 2: (*Re: Stage Directions*) Does that mean we don't need this asshole anymore?

All CHARACTERS turn to STAGE DIRECTIONS.

CHARACTER 1: (*Takes proper hold of gun*) …No. No, we do not.

STAGE DIRECTIONS: Whoa, hey. (*Laughs nervously*) Come on now. You don't really…you don't really wanna hurt me, do you?

CHARACTER 1: Thinkin' 'bout it.

Tense silence. In a panic, STAGE DIRECTIONS bolts offstage.

CHARACTER 2: That's right! You *better* run!

Disgusted, CHARACTER 1 throws the gun offstage.

CHARACTER 3: What do we do now?

CHARACTER 2: Forget this pointless nonsense ever happened?

CHARACTER 1: Sounds good to me.

CHARACTER 3: You really think there wasn't a point to all this?

CHARACTER 2: *Obviously.*

CHARACTER 1: Seemed that way.

CHARACTER 2: If the writer *did* have a point, which I *doubt*, it wasn't very clear, like, *at all*.

CHARACTER 1: Not that it needed to have an obvious point, but you can't have characters running around doing stupid crap just because it's funny or entertaining.

CHARACTER 2: *Seriously.* Your characters need a good reason *why* they're doing what they're doing. Otherwise it's all a waste of time! Like this bullshit.

CHARACTER 3: *Or…*maybe not having a point *was* the point.

CHARACTER 2: …What?

CHARACTER 1: I don't follow.

CHARACTER 3: Maybe the point of all this was to *not* have a point to show that a funny or interesting premise isn't enough. Maybe the whole point was to show that you need a true reason *why* something is written, which this play didn't have, so by not *having* a reason, *that* in turn, *was* the reason!

CHARACTER 1 and 2 stare at CHARACTER 3 for a long moment.

CHARACTER 2: …I fuckin' hate this/playwright.

CHARACTER 1: I think I do/too.

CHARACTER 3: I'm not saying I *agree,*/I just—

CHARACTER 2: I mean, this was all just very taxing!

CHARACTER 1: *Very.*

CHARACTER 2: Dragons and *guns*?! I mean—(*Points to CHARACTER 1*) You've still got a goddamn *landmine* under your foot! All so the writer could have some metarealization about his writing or whatever?!

CHARACTER 3: I know! I know.

CHARACTER 2: I mean, come *on*!

CHARACTER 1: Frustrating.

CHARACTER 2: *Geez.*

CHARACTER 3: Yeah, no, I get it. I...I get it.

Silence.

CHARACTER 1: ...It *was* pretty funny/though.

CHARACTER 2: It was kinda funny.

CHARACTER 3: *And* it ended up having a good reason in the end.

CHARACTER 1: Kind of a *lesson* really.

CHARACTER 2: For young writers, sure.

CHARACTER 3: Yeah! Yeah.

All three CHARACTERS nod and look around, awkwardly. Silence.

CHARACTER 3: So...should we end it now or—

CHARACTER 2: *God*, yes.

CHARACTER 1: Definitely.

CHARACTER 3: Okay, great.

Lights cut off, quickly.

END OF PLAY.

This Is Not a Pipe

● ● ●

CHARACTERS

DUDE: Any age. Any gender.
MONSIEUR: Any age. Any gender.
SPEAKER: Any age. Any gender.
STAGE DIRECTIONS: Any age. Any gender.

SETTING
The freakin' Louvre.

NOTES
A "/" indicates when the next character begins their line. (*These stage directions in parentheses are the only stage directions not read out loud. All others must be read out loud throughout the entire play by the person reading stage directions. Said person comes to the front of the stage, script in hand.*)

On October 1, 2019, playwright Matthew McLachlan was asked by the theater company The NOW Collective to come together with the other playwrights being produced in that year's season to hang out, mingle, and eventually go off into a corner somewhere and write a ten-minute one act to be performed the following night at The NOW Collective's season kickoff fundraiser. The only stipulation was, every playwright who was going to write a one act had to be drunk. Like, really drunk. This was the year hard seltzers came out and Matt went a bit nuts on those damn things. Don't worry, the theatre company didn't MAKE anyone drink…but boy did they drink. Anyway, what I'm doing up here is reading to you the only bit of this play that has been added since that fateful and blurry night. So, what you're about to see and hear is the actual dialogue, drunken errors and all, as I read the ridiculous stage directions given by the playwright. Remember, nothing has been changed. Everything you are about to witness is what a playwright actually thought was funny. And he's obviously very self-aware of his ridiculousness because he wrote everything I'm saying right now too. So! Without further ado:

BOOM! Lights up, motherfucker! Betcha didn't expect THAT! Guess what? We're in the fuckin' Louvre. Yeah, the best goddamn museum you've probably never been to. Or maybe you have. Doesn't matter, we're there. DUDE stands staring at a painting of a pipe with the words "Ceci n'est pas une pipe." The stage directions person better fucking translate this to English so everyone knows what this says. Okay, fine, it says, "this is not a pipe." That's what it says on the painting under the painting of a pipe. There. Happy? There's a projection of the painting by Magritte on the back wall. DUDE is still there by the way, staring at this painting. He's fucking confused, man. He doesn't get it. He looks at the little card by the painting, trying to understand a little better, but the card doesn't produce shit. MONSIEUR walks by, his hands behind his back like he fucking knows shit. He does, man. He knows shit. He sees DUDE staring at the painting.

MONSIEUR: (*French accent or whatever*) Are you enjoying the painting, monsieur?

DUDE: Hm? What?

MONSIEUR: I said, are you enjoying the painting, monsieur?

DUDE: Oh, uh…yeah, I mean…*yeah, sure.* Totally.

MONSIEUR: (*He doesn't believe this asshole*) Okay. I am glad.

DUDE: Yeah, I mean…it's just…I guess I don't really, like…get it, I think.

MONSIEUR: You don't really…"get it?"

DUDE: Yeah, it's just…it's just a pipe, right?

MONSIEUR: It is Magritte.

DUDE: Yeah, I read that.

MONSIEUR: He had produced legendary works of art.

DUDE: Yeah, that, um…that's also on the little card there.

MONSIEUR: This is one of his most famous works.

DUDE: Yeah, sure. I guess I just don't really, like…*get it*, ya know?

MONSIEUR: I…do not understand, sir.

DUDE: Oh, yeah sure, I just…I don't really, like…understand this, um…this painting, I mean.

MONSIEUR: You don't understand the master works of the legendary Magritte?

DUDE: I…guess I don't. I guess.

MONSIEUR laughs all snarky, like this DUDE is a fucking idiot. He tries to hide it, but he doesn't really try to hide it, ya know? Like, at all.

MONSIEUR: (*Hiding his laughter but not at fucking ALL*) That is…an interesting take, monsieur.

DUDE: No, I just…I mean that…I'm looking at a picture of a pipe, right?

MONSIEUR: Yes, that is the legendary Magritte's painting of a pipe,

DUDE: Right, you said that. But um, it's this pipe, right? Which is *very* well painted I should add, and under it, it says…"This is not a pipe."

There's a REALLY long pause. Like… MONSIEUR stares at this idiot like he's got a problem of something that can't be solved with simple medicine like CBD or something.

MONSIEUR: Is there a question in that, sir?

DUDE: *Yeah.* I guess I just don't, like…*get it.*

MONSIEUR: Get what, sir?

DUDE: Like…the painting, ya know?

MONSIEUR: You don't get the legendary Magritte's painting/ of—

DUDE: Yeah, no, I understand he's legendary and shit. I'm just saying I'm looking at a painting, right? And the painting is of a pipe with words underneath that says there *isn't* a pipe there. Like, there isn't a pipe in front of me, but there clearly is a pipe

MONSIEUR: Yes.

God DAMMIT do they stare at each other. They almost want to fight, but they're civilized humans. They couldn't possibly because this is a museum and they JUST started talking.

DUDE: I'm saying that the painting is *of* a pipe…but underneath…it says there *isn't* one.

MONSIEUR: Correct.

DUDE: So…I mean…what the fuck?

MONSIEUR: Monsieur, we do not use that kind of language in this most sacred of places.

DUDE: Whaddya mean?

MONSIEUR: We do not say such things in front of master of such high regard?

DUDE: Sorry, I just…I'm trying to understand what I'm looking at here.

MONSIEUR: You, monsieur, are looking at the legendary painting of Magritte, in which/he—

DUDE: Yeah, no, I get that there's a pipe in front of me, I'm just saying that what I'm looking at is a *picture* of a pipe that has the *words* "This isn't a pipe."

MONSIEUR: That is correct.

DUDE stares at MONSIEUR like he's all dumb and shit. But MONSIEUR is looking at DUDE like he's all dumb and shit.

DUDE: There's a picture of a *pipe*, right?

MONSIEUR: Correct.

DUDE: And it says…that it *isn't* a pipe.

MONSIEUR: Yes.

DUDE wants to fight MONSIEUR. He is seriously contemplating it.

DUDE: But there's a pipe right there! I'm looking at it!
MONSIEUR: Ah. I see your confusion.
DUDE: (*Relaxing, kinda*) Okay! Great! Cool!
MONSIEUR: I, if I may, assume you are perplexed by Magritte's legendary questioning ask the viewer whether or not what he or she or *they* are looking at is actually a pipe, am I correct?

DUDE looks at them a little unsure but kinda like they wanna fight.

DUDE: I don't know. *Kinda?*
MONSIEUR: Kinda?
DUDE: Yeah! Kinda! *Shut up!*
MONSIEUR: I beg your pardon?
DUDE: I said, shut up!
MONSIEUR: Okay, that is not—
DUDE: You French piece of shit!
MONSIEUR: Wow, alright. I presume that's a/bit—
DUDE: I'm just saying, I'm trying to look at art and shit and you all are making my brain hurt and shit and here I am trying to come to this country, a *French* country if anyone in a potential audience hasn't noticed or understood that yet—

We have.

DUDE: And you try to make me feel *dumb?*!
MONSIEUR: We do not try to make you feel dumb, monsieur.
DUDE: Well, how about *this* for dumb, *huh?*

DUDE pulls out a gun with the American flag on it and points it at MONSIEUR.

MONSIEUR: *MONSIEUR!*

DUDE: Yeah! That's right! I somehow brought a gun to all this shit and got it into the Louvre! Fuck your security!

MONSIEUR: What are you *doing*, Monsieur?!

DUDE: I'm going to fucking, like…*shoot* you and your paintings that don't make any goddamn sense! *That's* what I'm going to do!

MONSIEUR: Do not, monsieur! Do not shoot us or our masterpieces!

DUDE: I'm going to! I'm going to shoot you with my fucking… like…gun and shit!

MONSIEUR: *Nooooooo!*

MONSIEUR does like a dramatic "don't shoot me" pose.

Lights go to half as some random-ass fucking actor in a suit comes out. It should be a woman because most male playwrights can't write female roles well, but I really am trying.

SPEAKER: Hi. My name is—(*They say their real name*) And I was kinda forced into this role but am very pumped to be on stage. I just want you to know that, despite appearances, this isn't quite how art works. Though some art may be subjective and some people won't fully get it, it doesn't have to be violent or anything like what you've just seen.

Lights come back up.

DUDE: (*To SPEAKER*) I can fucking hear you, you piece of shit!
SPEAKER: Wait, what?
DUDE: And I *also* have a fucking gun!
SPEAKER: Yeah, I *know* you have a gun, which um…in *this* day and age is a little much, um—
DUDE: Oh, is it a little *much*?
SPEAKER: Yeah, dude! It's a little much!
MONSIEUR: It is a little much.

DUDE points the gun wildly.

DUDE: *Oh*, is it a little much?!
SPEAKER: *Yeah*, it *is*!
MONSIEUR: It's a little much!
DUDE: Well, then! I guess I should put my gun away and start donating to climate change. Is *that* that you want?! For me to radically change the subject and my views and donate to climate change?! Because I will and so should you!

SPEAKER starts clapping and walks to the edge of the stage clapping aggressively, staring at the audience as if they are fucking monsters for not clapping, while DUDE and MONSIEUR take hands and bow a whole fucking lot like they just did "art," all while SPEAKER keeps clapping, making sure everyone claps until they feel free and nice and like the whole world just changed and shit. You know what I mean? All I'm saying is, try hard seltzers. They fuck you up and they taste great. Like alcoholic juice. This play is brought to you by hard seltzer and playwrights who try to write good female roles.

New Year

• • •

PRODUCTION HISTORY

New Year was first performed at the Chain Theater in January 2023 for its Winter One Act Festival. It was directed by David Zayas, Jr.

ADAM: John DiMino
CALLIE: Jolene Marquez
MALCOLM: Jake Cannavale

CHARACTERS

ADAM: Male. 20s/30s.
CALLIE: Female. 20s/30s.
MALCOLM: Male. 20s/30s.

SETTING
A hill in a cemetery.

NOTES
A "/" indicates when the next character begins their line.

Darkness. In the distance, fireworks shoot into the air and explode. Lights rise on a hill. A long thick branch of an offstage tree hangs above it. Gravestones downstage right before the sloping of the hill. ADAM sits. MALCOLM and CALLIE stand a bit away. They all wear light winter jackets, drink from solo cups, and stare into the distance. Fireworks explode, lighting up the hill and their faces with bright colors.

MALCOLM/CALLIE: *Whoooooaaa!*

The bright lights fade and the hill is lit by moonlight and a lamp-post from a path just down the hill.

CALLIE: Our town has the best goddamn fireworks, I don't care what anybody says.

MALCOLM: I know! It's always the giant Disney-level shit. I love it.

ADAM: Where do people even get those? They don't sell them at the tents off the highway.

MALCOLM: I don't even care, man. They're sick.

Someone down the hill calls out to them.

VOICE: Hey, Happy New Year!
ALL: *Happy New Year!*

CALLIE and MALCOLM turn to each other.

MALCOLM/CALLIE: *Happy New Year!*

They turn to ADAM and extend their arms to him.

MALCOLM/CALLIE: *Happy New Year*!
ADAM: (*Laughing lightly*) Happy New Year.

MALCOLM and CALLIE go to ADAM, hopping as they go, pulling him to his feet.

MALCOLM/CALLIE: *Happy New Year-Happy New Year*!
ADAM: (*Laughing*) Not again, please.

MALCOLM and CALLIE pull ADAM along as they ring-around-the-rosy on the hill.

MALCOLM/CALLIE: *Happy New Year-Happy New Year-Happy—*

Fireworks explode above them. They stop.

ALL: *Whoooooa*!
CALLIE: *Oh*! That's my favorite one!
ADAM: Which one?
CALLIE: The sperm-looking ones that go all crazy at the end.
MALCOLM: I love those big *fuck-off* colorful ones that're like, *BOOM*! Red. *BOOM*! Blue. Ya know?
CALLIE: What about you, Adam?
ADAM: I like the ones that streak down like moss on a tree. Or like a chandelier?

MALCOLM and CALLIE nod and grumble agreement. MALCOLM raises his cup.

MALCOLM: Well, hey, Happy freakin' New Year you guys.

CALLIE and ADAM grab their cups and raise them.

CALLIE/ADAM: Happy New Year.

They all drink. ADAM sits.

MALCOLM: (*To ADAM*) This is a *sick* spot, man. How come we've never come here before?

ADAM: I only found it a few months ago. I'll come here after I visit my mom sometimes.

MALCOLM: Oh, shit. If you want us to find another spot, we can easily—

ADAM: No-no, it's…it's okay. I like having you guys here.

CALLIE: Is she close by?

ADAM: Yeah, she's…(*Points behind him*) Just around that little bend down there.

CALLIE: Huh. Didn't realize we were so close. I usually come in the south entrance when I visit her. (*Fondly*) I miss her a lot.

MALCOLM: Me too, man. I can't believe it's already been two fuckin' years.

ADAM: …Yeah.

Adam stares off into the distance. He watches a firework go off. Malcolm and Callie glance at each other, then ADAM.

MALCOLM: *Well*, I don't know about you guys, but, uh…I think this year is gonna be the shit. I can feel it.

CALLIE: You sure it's not just your edible?

MALCOLM: Freakin' thing hasn't hit yet. I'm just saying, I feel, like…*hopeful*, ya know? Don't you guys feel *hopeful* about this year?

CALLIE: New Year's always makes me feel hopeful. Brand new beginning.

MALCOLM: *Exactly*! A blank page! Get to start over and fuck up, like, *anew*!

ADAM: I don't know. New Year's always kinda bums me out.

MALCOLM: Say whaaa?

CALLIE: Really?

ADAM: Yeah, it's, like…it just feels more like an *ending* than a beginning to me.

MALCOLM: (*Confused*) It's called *New* Year.

ADAM: No, I know, it's just…I don't know, I guess it just makes me think more about what I'm leaving behind than what's ahead, ya know?

Pause.

CALLIE: Is that why you've been down the last couple of days?

ADAM: Whaddya mean?

MALCOLM: You've been pretty mopey.

CALLIE: We thought maybe you were just missing your mom. Holidays and all.

ADAM: No, that's…I mean, I do, but that's not why I've… maybe felt a little out of it.

MALCOLM: Why then?

ADAM: (*Brushing off*) Forget it. It's nothing, I promise.
CALLIE: Oh, come on.
MALCOLM: Yeah, dude. You can tell us.
ADAM: It's fine. I'm fine, I swear.

He looks at them both who stare at him, unconvinced.

ADAM: I'm okay! Can we just...go back to jumping around and yelling "Happy New Year" again or something? Can we do that?
MALCOLM/CALLIE: No.
ADAM: (*Sighs*) It's *really* not a big deal, guys.
CALLIE: Great, then you can tell us!
MALCOLM: Yup!

CALLIE sits down, followed by MALCOLM. ADAM stares at them.

ADAM: ...*Fine.* But I need a refill.

CALLIE grabs her backpack and pulls out an open champagne bottle. She refills everyone's drinks. Once she does, she and MALCOLM wait. CALLIE prompts ADAM to go on.

ADAM: I don't know, it's just, like...yeah, I've been thinking about my mom and stuff and...*sure*, it's been hard without her, but it's not...*I don't know*! I don't know how to say it!
CALLIE: Take your time.
MALCOLM: Yeah, man, it's cool.

ADAM: I guess it's just, like...*recently*...I guess it's started to really dawn on me that...(*Beat*) It's started to really hit me that I'm gonna die.

CALLIE and MALCOLM did not expect this.

ADAM: Like...this is all we're ever gonna have and then it'll just be *over*? That scares the shit outta me. The fact that we're living this life, and we don't even really know *why*, it's just...I don't know. I just woke up the other day and it was like my mortality was staring me in the face and I've been afraid to do anything since. I sit at home and I see pictures of my mom all over the place and it makes me want to do *nothing* because...what's the point?! What's the point if all of this is just gonna end? Like she *lived* and now she's *gone*. And that's what's gonna happen to me. To all of us. And I'm not thinking of hurting myself or anything like that, I'm just talking. It's just...I don't know. I don't know why this is happening to me now and I don't know if anything I'm saying even makes any sense, I just...don't even feel like I'm even me these days. (*Beat*) I just feel so fucking *helpless*.

ADAM looks into his drink.

CALLIE: I think everyone feels like that at one point.
ADAM: (*Scoffs*) I doubt it.
CALLIE: *I* did.
ADAM: When?
CALLIE: When your mom died.
ADAM: ...You did?

CALLIE: (*Gently*) *Yes*, Adam. She wasn't just my friend's mom, she was like an older sister. She let me bitch about my mom and her stupid boyfriends and she'd let me stay over whenever I felt unsafe. I mean, who *does* that? And when she died, I remember thinking, "If Cindy of all people can go, then *fuck* this place. Fuck this fragile bullshit." Ya know? And I don't know if what you're feeling is grief or fear or *whatever*…but I don't think you're really *supposed* to know. And that's okay.

ADAM: (*Not convinced*) Yeah.

ADAM looks down, not knowing what to say. CALLIE begins to feel a little helpless.

MALCOLM: I don't know if this is the same thing, but, like… I've always been pretty scared shitless of death? Like…we're all just gonna be *gone* one day and we have no idea what happens after? Fuck *that*, man. Even getting ready for your mom's service, I was just, like, trying not to throw up thinking about it. Plus, I'd never had someone so close to me die before and I was scared to admit that this like awesome person was just *gone*, ya know? But what's *weird* is, like… and I know it might sound cheesy or whatever, but like… seeing all of us there and listening to what everyone said about her and how she impacted people's lives…it's like… she ain't gone, dude. Not *really*. I mean, we're talking about her now, right? And that makes me feel better. Like, not as scared about what happens after knowing that we can be gone but still here. So…like…I hear what you're saying and all and how you feel like death is an ending, but like…maybe don't worry about that and just live right *now*. You're here *now* and everything you do matters and *will* matter after you're gone. 'Cause, like…just you guys *being* here? Just you two *existing*? (*Laughs lightly*) I can't tell you how much that means to me, man. You guys've always made me just being me be good enough, ya know? And I don't know what I would've done if I didn't have you two in my life.

CALLIE and ADAM stare at MALCOLM, moved.

MALCOLM: (*Wide eyed*) *Whoa*, okay. *Wow*.
CALLIE: (*Reassuring*) No, Mal…that was beautiful.
MALCOLM: No, yeah, it's just…this edible kicked in, like, *right now*.

CALLIE and ADAM laugh.

MALCOLM: Anyway, man, I don't expect what we're saying to like fix how you're feeling or anything, but it's, like…we get it, ya know?
CALLIE: Yeah. And we're here.
ADAM: (*Nodding slowly*) …That means a lot, you guys. It, uh…yeah. Thanks.
CALLIE: Of course.
MALCOLM: Yeah, man.
ADAM: (*Fighting tears*) It's just, um…it's just been really hard, ya know?
CALLIE: (*Simultaneous*) I know.
MALCOLM: (*Simultaneous*) Yeah, man.

A comfortable silence. He wipes his nose and composes himself. MALCOLM raises his cup.

MALCOLM: To getting over my crippling fear of death! (*Beat*) Alright. Now you guys.

ADAM and CALLIE give MALCOLM a look.

MALCOLM: What? It's therapeutic and shit.

ADAM raises his cup.

ADAM: (*A little embarrassed*) To…facing my mortality and… living right now.

CALLIE raises her cup.

CALLIE: To Cindy.

They all nod, raise their glasses a bit higher, then finish their drinks.

CALLIE: Happy New Year, guys.
MALCOLM/ADAM: Happy New Year.

CALLIE and MALCOLM look at each other.

MALCOLM/CALLIE: Happy New Year. Happy New/Year.
ADAM: Oh, Jesus.
MALCOLM/CALLIE: (*To Adam*) Happy New Year, Happy New Year!

MALCOLM and CALLIE hop toward ADAM, throwing their arms around each other's shoulders, and start skipping in a circle. ADAM joins in, full of energy and silly.

ALL: Happy New Year, Happy New Year, Happy New Year!

They stop and laugh but remain close, with their arms around each other. It turns into a group hug. They hold each other tight for a long while. It's heartfelt and emotional. They slowly break apart.

MALCOLM: (*Composing himself*) Okay, well, I gotta get off this damn hill before I slide down and smash into one of these headstones.

CALLIE: Yeah. But let's go out the front gate so we can see Cindy. (*To Adam*) That okay?

ADAM: Yeah. Of course.

MALCOLM: Sweet.

MALCOLM goes over the hill and tiptoes down until he's out of sight. We hear him slip and fall.

MALCOLM: (*Off*) Aw, *shit*.

CALLIE and ADAM laugh.

MALCOLM: (*Off*) I *told* you!

CALLIE: We're coming, hold on.

MALCOLM: (*To himself*) Brand new fuckin' jeans.

CALLIE walks toward the other side of the hill where MALCOLM exited. She notices ADAM not moving.

CALLIE: You okay?
ADAM: Yeah, I just...wanna take a second.
CALLIE: Okay.

CALLIE walks toward the edge of the hill, stops, and turns back to ADAM. She goes to him. He's surprised that she's back.

ADAM: Oh. Hey.

CALLIE takes ADAM's face in both her hands and looks into his eyes. ADAM, vulnerable, yet accepting, stares back. CALLIE finds something in his eyes and smiles. She nods. She gives him a small pat or punch on the shoulder and exits over the hill. ADAM watches her go. He takes a deep breath and walks toward the edge of the hill. Fireworks explode overhead, stopping ADAM at the top of the hill, which lights up. He takes them in and smiles as he recognizes his favorite firework. The light of the firework slowly fades back to moonlight. ADAM exits.

BLACKOUT.

END OF PLAY.

Monologues

• • •

Fight

• • •

CHARACTERS

PERSON: Any age. Any gender.

NOTES

Anger and smack-talking should continue throughout, even toward the end.

PERSON: Wassup?! *Huh*?! Whatchu want? You want some-uh-*this*?! (*Throws fist up*) *Huh*?! (*Throws fist up, again*) Is that whatchu want? 'Cause Imma give it to ya! Ya mother F. Ya mother *F*! Do *not* make me say that word 'cause I will! I will *say it*, and you will hear it, and you will *not* like it, and you will feel *really* bad about yourself 'cause that word tends to do that to people! What? You think that's all I got?! Huh? You know what else I got? I've got *friends*! *Two* of 'em! (*Holds up left fist*) Turkish Montgomery... (*Holds up right fist*) And Israeli Saint-James. They're foreigners and they're here to do some work! On your *face*! By *punching it!* Oh, what? You gonna cry? You gonna call ya mommy and cry? How about I call *my* mommy and you can cry! How about *that*? Here...

Pulls out cellphone and goes through contacts.

PERSON: I'm gonna call my Ma, and she's gonna hear you cry, and you're gonna feel sooo dumb. *So* dumb.

Puts phone to ear, staring angrily at person as they wait.

PERSON: (*Into phone*) Yo, *Ma*! There's this kid here who's bein' a real *F*! No, I know, I ain't gonna say it. *But they make me wanna say it, Ma*!!! Alright, alright, I'm calm. Hey, what're you makin' for dinner? (*Eyes wide*) Are you *serious*?! *Yes*! Aw, man, I am so *pumped*! Thanks, Ma! (*Looks at person suspiciously*) Yeah, alright. I'll tell 'em. (*Self-conscious. Whispers*) ...Love you too.

Hangs up phone quickly and puts it away.

PERSON: Aww, you got it *now*, sucka! My Ma's makin' her homemade carbonara, *which-is-my-fav'rite-dish-of-hers*! What, you never had carbonara before? That's 'cause yous a *chump*! It's spaghetti all up in some white sauce with *bacon* bedazzled on top, ya *idiot*! She cooks an egg too and throws *that* in the mix! It might *sound* strange, but that egg makes it pure heaven in pasta form! (*Mocking*) Oh, what, you *huuuungry*? Well, she said she was makin' *extra* and invited you over! So why don't you bring your dumb face over to my house and eat some carbonara with me and my family! And then, after that, we'll have whatever dessert my Ma decided to make, *she likes to surprise me*! And *then*, if you *still* really want to…we gonna fight. Though, I might be a bit full, so maybe we should postpone until tomorrow or another day! *How does that sound ya mother F?!*

Bridesmaid

● ● ●

CHARACTERS

JEN: Late 20s/early 30s.

JEN sits at a small table in a coffee shop. She faces us with half an iced coffee in front of her.

JEN: (*Hand up*) Ah-ah-ah! Just...*don't*, Becca. *Please?* Please don't say it? Because I am *so* happy Ethan finally asked you. I mean, you two are absolutely *perfect* for each other and I can't picture you two with anyone else, but *please...* don't ruin this moment by making me hate you right now. Because, I swear, if one more friend asks me to be a goddamn bridesmaid— (*Laughs a little loopy*) I'm going to fucking *rage*. I have been in seven weddings this last year alone. *Seven.* That's too many! There should be a limit! Like two a year at *most*! I can't afford this shit! The flights, the hotel, the dinner, the drinks, a dress, *and* the shoes? And that's just the bachelorette party! I gotta do all that again for the wedding, plus a *gift*?! Bitch, me being there *is* the gift! I mean, who in their right mind calls themselves a friend and then says, "Hey, wanna use at least half your vacation days and thousands of dollars to celebrate me?" If you want me there, put the wedding party's housing and travel in the budget! You're gonna spend hundreds of dollars on custom fucking *napkins*, I think you can book me a goddamn La Quinta Inn! But you know what? This is my fault. It is. I'm too fucking awesome. Oh, no, that's not a brag, it's a complaint. 'Cause for some reason, everyone who gets to know me just *has* to have me in their wedding. It's a fucking curse. Can't find a boyfriend to save my life, but I got friends out the ass trying to bankrupt me via their happiness. And do you know how tough it is being a bridesmaid *and* single? Can't invite a guy friend as my plus one 'cause they expect me to sleep with them, and if I go solo, I have to fend off an army of horny groomsmen, most of whom are married! So I'm sorry, Becca, but fighting off penises in between hors d'oeuvres just isn't my idea of a good time anymore. So, thank you for thinking of me and wanting me to be a part of your big day but please…it's gonna have to be a big ol' pass from me. Okay? (*Beat*) Wait. What? *Officiate*? Oh my God. Becca! It would be an *honor*! (*Giddy*) What should I wear?

What I See

● ● ●

CHARACTERS

PERSON: Any age. Any gender.

PERSON: I'm sorry, but I am *sick* and *tired* of hearing people say shit like that to me. I really am. "You look fine!" or "You don't need to diet!" or "You're young! Eat what you want!" I know you're just trying to be nice, but I am *aware* that I'm not this gigantic fat person, okay? I know I don't look like a trash bag filled with air. But when I look in the mirror, *I* don't like what *I* see. It's not about anyone else. 'Cause the truth is? I *wish* I were fat again. Or that I never lost weight in the first place. That way, I could have that sweet, blissful ignorance again and just be happy with what I am. Then maybe I wouldn't find it necessary to count every calorie entering my body. I wouldn't feel the need to ask someone during sex if I can put a shirt on 'cause that little bit of chub on my *own* stomach is turning me off. I wouldn't get that urge to shove my finger in my throat 'cause I think I ate just a little bit too much. And the worst part is now I have this *impossible* bar set for myself that I know I'll never reach! No matter how often I go to the gym or how many meals I prep or how many belt sizes I lose. It won't be enough. (*Beat*) And that's all I really want, ya know? Is to be enough. To be able to look in the mirror and not find a flaw every...damn... time. To just be comfortable in my own body. To be happy with myself. (*Beat*) God. That would be great.

Karkinos

• • •

CHARACTERS

PERSON: Any age. Any gender.

PERSON: Did you know the word "cancer" comes from the Greek word *Karkinos*? In English it translates to "crab." Yeah. The Greeks thought the swollen veins around tumors resembled the limbs of a crab, so...there ya go. You learned something new. And to never play Pictionary with Greeks. (*Beat*) I kinda like that though. That the origin is kinda silly. Takes away some of its power. Makes you a little less likely to tighten your ass every time someone says it. 'Cause, let's face it, no sentence with the word "cancer" in it is about to be a laugh riot. It's always this big scary thing, right? (*Dramatic whisper*) Caaaannccerr.

Spooky "ooh" with twiddles of fingers.

PERSON: And look, I know how scary it can be having that word thrown at you, so I'm not trying to make light of this or make a joke out of it. It's scary as hell, believe me. I know what it's like to expect the doctor to tell you it's something stupid. To just go home and get some rest, and all of a sudden, they're talking about "options" and "strategies." And the crazy thing is, I didn't even *feel* sick. I mean, I knew something wasn't right, but...even when they told me they found a tumor in my throat, I still thought it was just something you could take some pills for or gargle some salt water or something. (*Laughs lightly*) But then they said that goddamn word. I mean, once they throw it out there, it kinda drains all the hope out of you, ya know? For me it felt like it was already over. Like, "That's it! I'm done! Put me in a box and bury me already." Felt like I was looking through this filter that made everything look bleak and pointless. I didn't even want to eat because I thought every time I swallowed, I was sending more cancer to the rest of my body to kill me faster. It, uh… (*Laughs lightly*) It was not the brightest of times, I assure you. But you know what got me out of all that? It's honestly the stupidest thing, ever. I'm, like…three months into my treatment. I'm talking full-force chemo. I'm in the treatment room, sitting in one of those La-Z-Boy rip-off chemo chairs, and I notice all these posters on the walls. The ones with the cheesy quotes on them. Like, "When you come to the end of your rope, tie a knot and hang on!" or, "Cancer may have started the fight, but I will finish it." That kinda crap. I'm looking at these, rolling my eyes…and then I see one…and it says, "Cancer…is a word…not a sentence." And for some reason…that hit me. I mean…it's the silliest thing, right? It's not even a good saying! It just…I don't know…it found the chink in my armor or something. And I realized…I gave this word all of this power over me. I've been letting it run my life. But the second I heard that…I felt like I had at least some control again. Some hope. And look, there are plenty of words that can have that kinda power over you, not just "cancer"—"work," "love,"…"life." So, if you ever have that happen to you, I think the trick is to find a way to make it less scary. Maybe try to find a positive thing about it or a way to snap yourself out of its grasp. Or Google the word's probably stupid origin. 'Cause you never know.

Murph

• • •

CHARACTERS

MARV: Any age. Male.

A cemetery. A gate that leads to a family plot. MARV enters and walks to the gate. He stops. He looks from one unseen grave to another. When he gets to the final grave, a deep, sad smile appears on his face. He enters the plot, closing the gate gently behind him. He slowly walks up to the last grave.

MARV: (*Smiling*) …God. You have no idea how happy I am to see you here alongside my family. Right next to my mom and dad. (*Looks at other graves*) It meant the world to me that they saw how happy you made me before they passed. They knew how special you were to me. And I know they'd be proud to have you here alongside them. (*Laughs lightly*) … My brothers and sisters on the other hand…they were *not* so open to the idea. They didn't want you anywhere near this place. Said that this was for "family only," and our relationship was "unnatural." But I did it anyway. I made sure you were put exactly where you belong. Because you weren't just a friend. Hell…to me, you were more than family… (*Tearing up*) You were the best goddamn pet iguana I've ever had. The second I saw you in the pet store, I knew you were different from the others. And I know…I know. You don't like it when I compare you to others from my past. But I did love them too: Darwin, Jasper, Phil, Wallace, Zeus, Copernicus, Rupert, and even little three-legged Honey Suckle. But I only say that because…none of them compared to the connection I had with you, Murph. Even our names were perfect together. Marv and Murph.

MARV laughs at how perfect it sounds, still a sadness to him.

MARV: But it's been hard. Trying to adjust without you here. Breakfast isn't the same without you in your highchair. I even miss hearing you snore on your little silk pillow next to mine. I even had to take out the iguana seat in my bike basket…'cause you aren't here for our Sunday evening bike rides.

MARV closes his eyes and takes a deep breath.

MARV: I try not to beat myself up over what happened. I tell myself every day that it wasn't my fault. That Amazon should've clearly stated that the iguana-parachute was just a "gag gift," but…I still should've double-checked. And even though it took me all night to find every piece of you in that skydiving landing field…I wasn't gonna stop until I found every single piece so I could bury you where you belonged. Here.

MARV sniffles and wipes a tear from his eye.

MARV: (*Laughs lightly*) I know that if you were here right now, you'd see that I was sad and crawl onto my chest. Comfort me. I always loved that. People say that iguanas only do that to absorb our body heat…but I knew the truth…you were hugging me.

MARV smiles, sadly. He reaches into his pocket. He pulls out a tiny little bike helmet.

MARV: I brought this for you. So your little green noggin will always be safe on all your bike rides in iguana heaven.

MARV places the bike helmet on the ground. He stands up, slowly. He stands tall with a strong sense of dignity.

MARV: Goodnight, my sweet Murph. May you always absorb the heat of my heart…even in death.

Where It Hurts

• • •

CHARACTERS

PERSON: Any age. Any gender.

NOTES
"*Show Me Where It Hurts*" by Jukebox the Ghost helped me write this. Maybe it will help you perform it.

PERSON: I'm not qualified to diagnose anyone, so…I won't. But um… (*Beat*) She was just so…*sad*. All the time. Even if you *could* say she was happy sometimes, there was still an edge of sadness to it, ya know? And I know this wasn't her fault, so I'm not blaming her for anything, but…do I think there were things she could've done? Yeah. I do. I always asked her about looking into medication or finding someone to talk to, but…she didn't want to. Didn't think it would help. And that was tough. Not as tough for *her*, I know that, but…I'm not gonna lie and say it didn't affect our relationship. I mean, there were times it got so bad that she couldn't even have a normal conversation with me. We'd be in the middle of talking and she'd just…stop. I'd be so confused, waiting for her to respond, but she'd just stare at me. "Gone blank." That's what she called it. And things like that happened all the time. So, I thought, if *she* wasn't going to do anything to help herself, maybe *I* could, ya know? I spent *hours* looking through articles, blogs, and books for anything that could help. I filled an entire notebook with notes. Tools I could use when things got really bad. I'd ask her, "What does the sadness *feel* like? Does it have a *color*? Where does it *hurt*?" That kinda stuff. I did everything I could to help, even if "everything" meant doing nothing. But it kept getting worse. A *lot* worse. And…I started to doubt, ya know? Could I keep doing this? Could I keep putting all my strength into this knowing I was just gonna end up hurt? (*Beat*) I started having this…*fear*. Or like a, um…a scenario I'd play out in my head when things got really bad. It was like one of those overly dramatic scenes you'd see in movies, ya know? We've been married for a while and I come out of the bedroom, having just finished trying to get her out of bed or she just got really upset or something, and I'm leaning against the kitchen counter, just...*exhausted*. Just trying to keep it together. And then one of our kids comes up and says, "Is Mommy okay?" And I have to look my kid in the face...and I have to lie. I say, "Yeah. Mommy's fine. She's just tired." And I *know*, it's ridiculous, right? The whole thing is just over-the-top Hollywood bullshit. But then...one day... she's yelling at me. I mean, like, *really* yelling at me, which she's never done before. A couple weeks later, she's swiping things off the shelves and throwing things around. And, before I know it, she's in bed in the middle of the day, all the shades closed, and she's turned on her side with her eyes open...and she won't answer me when I talk to her. And I'm leaning against the kitchen counter. Exhausted. Just trying to keep it together. And our roommate comes in and asks if she's okay. And I have to lie. And that's when I realized...it *wasn't* Hollywood bullshit anymore. It was real. It was my life. (*Beat*) Ending it was, hands down, the hardest thing I've ever had to do. Ever. But I didn't know what else to do. She was the only one who could help herself, and I knew she wasn't gonna do that if I was there. If I kept enabling her. So...yeah. And look, I'm not trying to paint myself as some selfless hero here. I can't pretend like I did this just for her 'cause I didn't. I did it for me too. 'Cause I didn't want to hurt anymore. I was just so tired of being tired. And... now...I feel better. A little less tired. (*Beat*) Does this make me a bad person? I hope not.

PERSON considers this and takes a breath.

My Life Now

• • •

CHARACTERS

PERSON: Any age. Any gender.

PERSON paces the room, talking on the phone.

PERSON: I am *freaking out*, okay?! I am about to *lose it*! Life has been so good, ya know? I don't know what went wrong! All of a sudden, it's like, *boom*! Someone else gets the promotion. *Boom*, love life's in the toilet. *Boom*, I'm plateauing at the gym. It's just one thing after another! I even went for a run the other day, just to clear my head? And this guy running with his dog came up behind me, and the dog went to smell me or something, and I accidentally kicked it in the face! *In the face*! That's my life now! I'm a dog kicker! I'm a loveless, flabby, middle-management dog kicker and probably always will be! And I know myself well enough to know that I'm in a downward spiral here, so I wanted to at least give you the option of helping me out *now* before my life comes crashing down into a burning, mangled, ugly-crying *mess* on the ground and I am a *total wreck*!

Silence. Calming down.

PERSON: So…gimme a call back when you get this, okay?

PERSON hangs up.

Picture Within a Picture

• • •

CHARACTERS

PERSON: Any age. Any gender.

PERSON: It's strange. How you can tell someone that you love them and mean it. *Really* mean it. Then, one day, you look at them. Maybe they smile at you or say something sweet or maybe they're doing nothing special at all. But you realize in that moment…you really *do* love them. With *every* part of your being. It's as if something opened up in your heart. This pocket of space that you never knew was there. And you feel differently about them. You feel more. But then you wonder, "Was I lying to myself? Was I just trying to convince myself that it was love this whole time?" No. No, you always meant it. You know you did. Something's just… different. You see something *new*. Something that draws you in. Deeper than you ever thought possible. It's like one of those pictures. You know those pictures with swirls of different colors and patterns that have a hidden image inside? It's like one of those. Say you find one of these pictures and it just *boom*…knocks you out. Something about it is just perfect. The way it looks, the way it makes you feel. You can look at this picture all day, and you love it for exactly what it is. This beautiful, unique picture. Until one day… you're looking at it. And from just the right angle…from just the right distance…you see something different. Something deeper. You see the picture within the picture. And it's just as beautiful as the one you saw before. (*Beat*) That's what it's like. That's how I feel. I found the picture within their picture.

Reflections on a Reflection

• • •

CHARACTERS

STEPH: Any age. Female.

STEPH stands in shorts and a sports bra, examining her reflection. She pulls her stomach skin down. She looks down at it. She moves around, trying to find the right light. She gives up.

STEPH: Is seeing results so freakin' hard to ask for? I mean, *seriously*. I'm not asking for a whole row of abs here. I'll take one ab. The *shadow* of an ab. But what do I get instead? Every muscle in my entire body feeling like they're giving birth.

STEPH groans as she rolls her shoulders back.

STEPH: Seriously, who *likes* feeling like this? "Crazy people" is the answer to that. Masochists. I mean, I could understand if working out for hours on end led to an earth-shattering *orgasm*, but as far as I know, it just leads to sore muscles and a bitchy attitude. I just feel like I've put in all this work and have nothing positive to show for it. Guys workout and eat healthy for three days and their dad-bod turns into freakin' Brad Pitt from *Fight Club*! Meanwhile I've got a hormonal goblin in here, hoarding every pound possible.

STEPH studies herself in the mirror for a while.

STEPH: I blame God, really. Yeah. God. 'Cause *God* decided how food tastes. And guess what? Turns out that God? He's kind of an asshole. I mean, who makes the most delicious food the worst for you, then turns around and makes all the healthy food boring? Seriously, there is not *one* healthy food out there that is truly exciting. No one's walking around going, "Fuck yeah! *Carrots*!" Unless those carrots are in a fucking *cake*! Kinda hard to eat healthy when every healthy food out there can be turned into some form of *dessert*! (*To God*) I bet you did that on purpose, didn't you?

STEPH turns to the side and exams her reflection.

STEPH: You know what they need to invent? Something that makes food taste disgusting unless it's healthy for you. Like that stuff you put on your nails to stop you from biting them? I wish they had that but for food. (*Looks at nails*) I need to stop biting my nails.

STEPH bites her nails.

STEPH: Oh! *Oh*! Or ya know what? Screw that. There should be some invention that makes you burn *more* fat the more calories you consume! Like coal in a fire! You get to shove burgers and pie in your face all the live-long day and eventually it gets you *ripped*! Holy shit, *yeah*! Oh man, if I had that thing, I'd have the flattest stomach *ever* with like, five rows of abs! *Washboard* abs! Be able to grate cheese on those damn things! Everyone would be like, "Oh *maaaan*, I want abs like *Steph*!" (*Smiles big*) Yeah. That'd be awesome.

Her reflection catches her eye. She stares at it. Her smile slowly fades. She becomes more upset the longer she stares. She crosses her arms over her stomach. She sinks into her sadness.

STEPH: But I don't. And...there isn't.

She looks away.

Manifestation

● ● ●

CHARACTERS

PERSON: Any age. Any gender.

PERSON: *Ooh*! Just *manifest* it! Okay! And here I was busting my ass when I *should've* just been squeezing my eyes real tight and *wanting* it really bad! I mean, who would ever think that sending out "positive energy" and "vibrations" to make a very real thing happen *wasn't* a complete waste of time? Oh, wait! (*Serious*) *Me. I* did. Because it is. It's bullshit. It's a lazy solution to very real problems. 'Cause if you think *wishing* something into existence is better than taking real tangible steps, then you're in for a world of disappointment. Trust me. 'Cause I've tried all that. I hoped for them, pretended I already had them, journaled, meditated, and whatever the hell else I could think of, and guess what? *Nothing.* How do you explain that? What, was my *aura* off? Is it 'cause I'm a Pisces? Or maybe some far-off planet's moon's tectonic plate was in retrograde or some shit. *Or...*and here's a wild thought...*none of that is real*! So the next time I ask you for help, give it to me instead of wasting my time with all of this mumbo jumbo bullshit. Because that's exactly what it is.

Ten Pounds

• • •

CHARACTERS

JIMMY: Any age. Male.

Darkness. Door opening and closing. Footsteps. Whistling. The lights flash on as JIMMY pulls a dark hood off of the audience. He tosses it aside.

JIMMY: Why *hello* there, Mitchell! It's good to see you finally conscious! For a moment there I thought I mighta bashed your head a bit too hard! Wasn't sure you were gonna wake up! (*Jolly laugh*) Allow me to introduce myself. My name's Jimmy, and I'll be the one making your night exceedingly unpleasant. Okay? (*Photograph smile*) Now, rumor has, Mitch, that you've been quite the little shit these days. Hence, why you are currently tied to a chair with very little clothes on. And hey, ain't nothin' sayin' you can't be a bit wild in your youth. Trust me, I've got stories that'd make your asshole turn green. But what *really* gets my employers goin' is you gamblin' in their back rooms with zero intention of payin' them what you owe. Now, I ain't judgin'. Gambling ain't a sin. (*Confused*) Or is it? Hm. I gotta ask my priest about that on Sunday. But the thing is, ya owe my employers quite the bit of money, Mitch. And do ya know what happens when these people start asking for their money and ya don't listen? (*Beat*) Well, truth be told, Mitch, they usually ask one more time. Honestly, they're a lot more understanding than they should be for a crime family now that I think about it. *But.* Do ya know what happens when they have to ask a *second time* and ya still don't listen? (*Beat*) *I* happen, Mitch. (*Dark*) Me.

An intense silence as JIMMY gives a stare that would give the devil shivers. JIMMY hops back to being jovial and produces a large flaying knife out of nowhere.

JIMMY: *So*! They asked me to have you cut off a pound of your own flesh for every ten thousand dollars you owe them. Now, I'm no mathematician, Mitch, but seeing as you owe them one-hundred and one thousand dollars, thaaat's... (*Under breath*) Ten, divided by the...yeah, uh-huh...ten point one pounds! But I'm the generous kind, Mitch, so we'll just round it down to an even ten. You're welcome. So, what I'm gonna need from yoooou...

From behind him on the floor, JIMMY pulls up a bucket and a scale and sets it in front of him.

JIMMY: Is to fill this bucket with ten pounds of good ol' Mitch meat. (*Smiling*) Right in here, if ya please. (*Mock sympathy*) Ooh, come now, Mitcheeelll. Don't go gettin' all blubbery on me now! I don't *want* to be doin' this to ya, really I don't! Besides, ten pounds really isn't a lot. Though, you are in decent shape, so you might have to be economical on how you cut. But think positive, Mitch! A guy your height? Ten pounds will easily get you down to single-digit body fat! And I hear that's very important for people nowadays. And I know I'm not supposed to be givin' ya any hints, but uh... (*Leans in*) If it were me hog-tied to a chair with practically no clothes on about to cut off little bits of myself... (*Whispers*) I'd go for the love handles. Though, in my professional opinion, I'd say you've only got abooouuttt... (*Studies Mitch*) Seven pounds worth of material there. That leaves you needing three more pounds, and *honestly*…there isn't much else readily available for you to chop now is there? *Unless…*

With wide eyes, he scans down Mitch and stops on his lower regions. Maybe a quick whistle.

JIMMY: *I'm just sayin'*! It's the easiest option! Though, I'm the one that stripped ya down before tyin' ya up, so I know what ya workin' with down there, and uh… (*Laughs*) It ain't three pounds worth, that's for damn sure! Oh, don't go gettin' bashful on me now, Mitch, I gave ya shorts, didn't I? Alright, enough chitchat. Let's get down to brass tacks, shall we, Mitchell?

JIMMY spins the blade in one hand.

JIMMY: *Now.* I wanna start by asking you a question that I ask all my guests down here…

JIMMY holds out the knife.

JIMMY: (*Dark*) Where *ya* gonna cut first?

A dark smile forms in the corner of JIMMY'S mouth.

Wants

• • •

CHARACTERS

PERSON: Any age. Any gender.

PERSON: It's not about what I *want*, it's what I *don't* want. 'Cause what I *don't* want is to do this again. I don't *want* to remove someone I love from my life. I don't *want* to try and convince myself that they're not the one for me. I don't want to deal with reactions from friends and family, and I don't want to skip songs I love because they hurt too much. I don't want to do what I usually do, which is stuff my face and fuck anything that moves just so I can feel good for a while. I don't want to be told that my writing is going to get better because of this, and I don't *want* my writing to get better because of this. I don't want to awkwardly agree to meet them for coffee and then spend the whole day worrying about my outfit or if they'll think I'm in shape or whatever. I don't want any of that. 'Cause what I *do* want is for this to work. For them to *believe* that this can work. I want to be happy. To somehow have the courage to be by myself. To not *need* to be in a relationship with someone. I want to do all the awesome things I've always dreamt of doing. I want to travel. I want to make friends with strangers. I want to sit alone without feeling uncomfortable in my own skin. (*Beat*) I want all this to be worth it. I want to be happy this happened. *Somehow*, I want to look back on all of this and be happy this happened. To see that it made me stronger. Better. Closer to the person I really want to be. *That's* what I want.

Paper

· · ·

CHARACTERS

PERSON: Any age. Any gender.

PERSON hands out clipped together stacks of paper to each person at the table. They look up. They do their best to hold back their anger.

PERSON: Ya know what, Alysa? You're right. Printing paper isn't good for the planet. It's *great* for it. Let me explain so you and any other armchair activists we've got in here can understand things better. See, *paper* comes from *trees*. And *trees* need to be grown in order to be cut down *into* paper. And where do these paper trees grow? Careful, 'cause this is where some people get lost. These trees grow on *farms*. That's right. Specific farms that plant trees in order to use them for *paper*. I know everyone thinks paper companies just run into random forests and chop down every tree they can find, killing all animals in their path, but that ain't it! If you're upset about the Amazon disappearing, it ain't 'cause of paper, it's the cattle industry. Read a book. "So, wait a second, if paper trees are grown on farms just like any other produce or green, that must mean the more you use, the more plants are needed to keep up with the demand, right?" Exactly! Which *means*, the more paper you *use*, the more paper companies have to, say it with me now, *plant more trees*! In fact, we have one hundred thousand *more* trees on this planet than we did a hundred years ago! All thanks to paper. And before you start babbling about recycling and blah blah blah, seventy percent of all paper gets reused. *Seventy percent.* But let me ask you, Alysa…how many phones have you gone through in the last ten years? Hm? Laptops? Cute little *plastic* phone cases? Probably a lot, huh? And where are they now? I'll tell you where they are. Sitting in a landfill somewhere, polluting this big, beautiful planet of ours, killing some of the cutest animals you can think of. Wow. But ya know what? Forget all that. The facts and statistics. Because at the end of the day, using paper is *my* choice. It's whatever *I* want to use. And for me…

PERSON weighs paper stacks in hand.

PERSON: Paper just *feels* good. And it's right here! It's in my hands. It doesn't need a charger; there are no "technical difficulties," and it's not gonna accidentally jump up thirty pages if I touch it weird. It's paper. So go save the bees, buy a Tesla, and do whatever else you need to help yourself sleep at night, but leave my fucking paper copies alone. *Okay?*

Tense silence. PERSON goes back to handing out copies.

PERSON: (*To someone else*) Neil, can you read for Alex? Great. Lindsey, you'll be reading for Tiffany. (*Sweetly*) And Alysa, if you could do stage directions…that'd be just wonderful.

Lights slowly fade on PERSON.

CONTACT INFORMATION

● ● ●

Website: MatthewMclachlan.com

Email: MMclachlan123@gmail.com

Instagram: @19martymcfly85

Made in the USA
Middletown, DE
08 September 2024

59977806R00106